Searching

Denise,
I admire you so much –
you are such a wonderful,
smart woman. Thanks to
you, here this is!
Barbara Wilkie

Searching

Barbara Wilkie

To order additional copies of this book, contact:
Xlibris Corporation
1-888-795-4274
www.Xlibris.com
Orders@Xlibris.com
91167

This book is dedicated to the three most important people in my life:
My husband, Gord, who has been brave enough to stay married to me for
over 24 years; and my parents, Clarence and Ella who continually tell me
they are proud of me and support me in all my many ventures.

CHAPTER ONE

H E SENSED THE man's presence a split second before the first blow landed on the back of his head. He staggered, and then twisted, as the huge shape loomed over him. Brant bent his arms over his head. The large fist slammed him a second time, then a third. Coppery blood spewed from his mouth. He fell to his knees. The big man kicked his ribs, knocking him sideways. Another kick landed on his kidneys; pain exploded in his body.

"Stack wants his money," the big guy growled. "When you gonna pay up? I gotta come back an' see ya?"

"No, no," Brant stammered, "tell him I'll have the money soon." He lay on his side, on the ground, his arms tight around his waist.

"See that you do. I don' wanna have ta come back after ya agin. Got it?" And just to make sure Brant got the message, the big guy gave one last savage kick to his back.

"O-kay," Brant managed to gasp.

After a few minutes, Brant slowly got to his feet, spitting blood, using his hands to push off the ground and then to slowly straighten, wincing at the bruises he could already feel forming. As he tried to take in a lungful of air, pain shot up his side where the brute had kicked him. What the hell was he going to do now?

As he stood there, hunched over like someone five times older, he tried to figure out what to do. He pushed his hair back out of his face and tried to think. After a few moments he tried standing a little straighter. It wasn't easy since every move made him wince and groan. He managed to straighten up enough so that he could walk and almost look like his normal six-foot height. With slow, managed breaths he made his way to the car and leaned against the fender until some of the ache eased.

Once behind the wheel, Brant went over his options. He didn't really have any deals on the go. It wasn't his fault he couldn't pick winners anymore. He was sure that last bet was going to come through for him. Now he was $20,000 in debt to Tim Stack. Brant's friends had told him Stack was bad news, but did he listen? No, of course not.

It had all started innocently enough though, during his senior year in high school. He'd overheard some of his friends talking about the football game from the night before and how much money they had made. Brant, who was broke, thought he'd give it a try. The first few months he had done quite well, and he was ahead by a few hundred dollars. Then his bets got bigger. Still, he managed to do okay until he got overconfident.

He'd never forget it.

It was the provincial basketball play-offs, and Brant was sure the home team would take it. The game was close until the last two minutes. He lost two thousand dollars on that game. Jessie, his sister, bailed him out and made him promise never to bet again, which of course he did. Made the promise and bet again.

Now, three years later, it was all catching up to him. Brant had managed to pay Stack enough to keep betting, but that was all over now. He slowly leaned his head against the headrest and tried to think of a way out. Everyone he knew was broke, at least when it came to that much money. He couldn't expect Jessie to bail him out yet again.

He started the car and pulled out onto the street.

After driving around aimlessly for a couple of hours, he still hadn't come up with a plan, so he decided to go to Tommy's Tavern, the local dive. As he got out of the car, his muscles groaned in protest. Gingerly, he straightened up and creaked into the bar.

Just inside the door, he stopped to look around and see whom he could see. Finally, there, through the smoke-filled room, he spotted a friend. As he walked by the bar, he ordered two beers, then he sat down across from Billy.

"Sit down, pal o'mine," Billy drawled, well on his way to being drunk.

"Don't mind if I do, Billy. How's it hangin'?"

"Not bad, not bad." Billy bobbed his head a few times and then stopped to take a closer look at Brant, squinting through the smoke. "Hey, you don' look so good. Looks like someone used you for a punchin' bag."

"Yeah, well, I got myself in some trouble with Stack. He sent one of his goons 'round to tune me up a bit." He looked at Billy with narrowed eyes, his look speculating. Billy was into some shady stuff now and then. Could he help? "Hey, do you know a way a guy could score some serious money?"

"How serious?" Billy asked, as he took a large swallow of beer.

"Put it this way, too much to earn working at Ernie's."

Billy looked at Brant, his forehead creased as he tried to think. After a few minutes of deep, beer-soaked thought, a sly grin formed on his face. "Well, I heard about some dope comin' into town," he told Brant, pinning him down with his eyes. "But no, it's too risky." Billy's eyes narrowed in challenge.

It didn't take long.

"What? Tell me. I'll decide what's risky."

"It's too risky!" Billy repeated, his lips twitching. "It's too risky because I heard the dope belongs to Stack!" He couldn't contain himself any longer and laughed out loud.

"Stack?" Brant repeated. The waitress finally showed up with the beer. Brant paid and handed one to Billy. "Cheers, man," he said, as he took a long drink. "That really hit the spot. Now, tell me more about this dope deal."

Billy blinked to clear the moisture from his eyes. "You gotta be kiddin'. I was just funnin' with ya! Rip off Stack? You'd be dead for sure." He shook his head.

Billy had a point. It would take dumb luck to be able to pull off a stunt like that. But if he didn't he'd be dead. There was no way Brant could come up with twenty grand and no other possibility for getting it.

"Come on, man," Brant pleaded, "I'm desperate."

"I can't believe this! You're nuts!" Billy shook his head. "Well, you didn't hear it from me." He proceeded to tell Brant all he knew. "It's supposed to be ten kilos of cocaine. You know this is dangerous. You could end up on a slab for this if they catch you."

"Yeah, I know. Thanks for the info." Brant stood up to leave. "Keep this between us."

"I'll come to your funeral, buddy." Billy saluted him with his beer bottle.

Brant had two days to come up with a plan. Armed with a map and the address Billy had given him, he drove around the area. Billy had told him it would happen in the alley. He found it during the day and went back that night to check it out again; it was perfect for his purpose. Streetlight barely penetrated the darkness.

There were lots of shadows and a dumpster to hide behind.

It was now time. Brant had stayed away from home for the last two days. He didn't want his sisters to figure out that something was going on.

Two blocks from the meeting place, he parked the car. He made his way to the alley and checked behind him every few seconds. As he entered the alley, he pulled out the 9mm handgun he'd brought.

The act of buying a gun had been easy. A friend of a friend had set him up with a dealer. They met in a deserted building on the edge of town. The man had shown him how to load and shoot it.

Brant looked at the gun in his hand. It made him nervous. All he had to remember was the money he owed and his courage came trickling back.

Billy had told him that the buy was supposed to be at midnight. It was now eleven-thirty. Brant hoped the gods were with him and the drugs would show up first. He hid behind the dumpster to wait.

Thirty minutes crawled by and still no one had shown up. Brant paced behind the dumpster; two steps forward, three steps back, then three steps forward and two steps back. His hands left moisture trails on the legs of his jeans. He was starting to shake with panic when a car finally pulled into the alley. He wiped each hand on his leg, carefully holding the gun, then gripping it tightly. The car had stopped but behind the dumpster he was blind. With trembling caution he stood, slowly, so he could peer over the top.

The vehicle came to a stop about ten feet away. A man climbed out of the car, then went to the trunk. He pulled out a large satchel then walked around to the front of the car and set it on the hood.

Brant gathered what courage he could and quickly searched the alley once more with his eyes. It was now or never.

The man turned away and looked down the alley. Brant crept out from behind the dumpster, his eyes wild, his breathing quick and loud. He ran up to the man with the gun extended, butt out, and clubbed him on the back of the head, then watched as the man grunted and fell.

Brant stood over the man and stared, frozen in place. It had actually worked! He shook his head to clear it then quickly bent to check for a pulse; the man was still alive but unconscious. He opened the satchel and saw ten packets of cocaine. He stared at all that powder and thought about the money it represented. He had one packet in his hand and was about to reach for another when he thought he heard a noise. He dropped the satchel and ran out of the alley.

Back out on the street he tried to act casual as he made his way back to the car. He had made it a block from the alley when he noticed a car moving slowly down the street toward him. It had to be Stack. Brant quickly ducked into a darkened doorway. As soon as the car was safely past, he left the doorway and ran to his car.

CHAPTER TWO

O NCE IN HIS car, he didn't waste any time getting away. A few blocks out of the area he pulled over. With trembling hands he pulled open his jacket and took out the packet. With his head lying against the headrest, he cradled the package as though it were a baby. He closed his eyes and took deep breaths until his heart rate slowed. Then he restarted his car and headed home, keeping the speedometer at a steady 48 KPH.

Now all Brant had to do was find a safe place to stash the package until he could find a buyer for it.

He pulled in the driveway, shut off the car, and sat there trying to think of a good hiding spot. He closed his eyes, and in his mind he went through the house room by room, closet by closet, but nothing jumped out at him. He should have figured this out ahead of time. With one hand on the car door and the other clutching the package of drugs, he had one foot on the ground when he spotted it.

It was perfect! An old Ford Escort, more rust than paint. He got out of his car and walked over to Jessie's car. The doors were unlocked, so he opened the driver's door to look around, but it was hard to see. He went back to his car and got the flashlight. With the beam pointed down, he looked in the front of the car, then the back. Jessie obviously hadn't been back here for a while. Food wrappers littered the floor behind the driver's seat. Still there didn't seem to be a spot good enough to hide a kilo of cocaine. He was about to give up when he backed into the open rear door.

He stood back from it and studied it, absently rubbing his thigh where the window crank had dug in to him. From the outside, it looked wide enough. He'd have to take the panel off and get a better look. As he checked the door panel for screws, a vehicle went by on the street. Brant hid the beam of his flashlight against his hand. He quickly looked up and down the street, all was clear. Brant closed his eyes as he waited for his heartbeat to slow down.

He opened his eyes and went to the trunk of his car to get the small toolbox. After a quick look up and down the street once more, he pulled a pair of needle-nose pliers and a flat-head screwdriver from the box. Back at Jessie's car, he used the pliers to remove the C-clip holding the window handle in place. Next he used the screwdriver to pry the panel away from the door. He rolled the window down; there was lots of room. He went back to his car and grabbed the package of cocaine and stuffed it into the bottom of the door. He put the panel back on, rolled the window down and up to double check that there weren't any problems. It worked! Carefully he closed the door. Even so, it still sounded like someone had slammed the door; he looked around and waited for lights to come on and people to investigate the noise, but no one did.

Finally in the house, he made his way to his room where he collapsed on the bed. It had been a long night and he was exhausted. He should have been able to fall asleep right away. Instead, he lay awake most of the night.

The next day, Brant started the next stage of his plan: finding a buyer. You would think that would be fairly simple in today's world, since there are so many people using illicit drugs. But how many people are trying to sell drugs to the people who sell drugs for the person you stole the drugs from? It just makes things a little more difficult. And if you're not a drug user yourself it's that much harder. Brant talked to some of his friends whom he knew were involved with drugs. They all told him about the same person: Jason Dickie.

Jason Dickie did not have a very good reputation. Brant's friends told him he was mean on his good days and no one went near him on the bad days. The more Brant tried to find someone else to go to, the fewer options he found until he realized Dickie was going to be his best, and probably only, shot.

Brant finally tracked him down, or rather his "secretary," and made an appointment for that evening. He spent the afternoon trying to calm his nerves. Ernie, his boss, had sent him home early from work since he wasn't much good in the state he was in. Between wondering how Stack reacted to the theft and preparing for the evening meeting, Brant was behaving as if he were in need of a fix himself.

Finally, it was time to meet with Dickie.

CHAPTER THREE

BRANT PULLED UP in front of an old, run-down apartment building. Dickie would be on the fourth floor. He went in the building. There was no security to speak of, so he just walked in the main door. The entry way was dimly lit and smelled of stale cooking and other strong, unidentifiable odors. He looked around for an elevator, and when he couldn't find one, he headed for the stairs. By the time he got to the fourth floor, he was out of breath despite his good physical condition. He stopped for a minute, took a deep breath, smoothed back his long, dark hair and approached the door of apartment D6.

His nervousness made the first knock faint. On the next try he got a response. He opened the door slowly, hesitantly, and was almost knocked over with the smell of unwashed bodies and spent drugs. Through the smoky haze he saw a stumpy man standing in a doorway. He had a gun in his hand. Brant threw his hands in the air.

"Who the fuck're you?" Dickie squinted at him, his comb-over sliding down his oil slicked forehead.

"I'm the guy Jeff told you about? I got some stuff to unload. You Dickie?"

"Yeah, that's me, so what? I ain't ever seen ya afore. How do I know you're not a narc or somethin'?" Dickie stepped forward to pat him down. "Turn around," he snarled. Brant complied. "Okay, you're clean. Put your damn hands down an' come in an' close the bloody door."

Brant took a step forward and closed the door. He watched Dickie warily as he sat in an old chair. The stuffing was falling out of it. Dickie motioned Brant to sit on the sofa across from him.

"So what's this stuff you got to unload? Better be worth my while."

"I've got a kilo of cocaine." He rubbed his hands on his legs, eyes darting around the room.

"One kilo, huh. Well, where did a shitwad like you get your hands on that much blow?"

"Does it matter?" He wiped his hands again. He'd never done this before. Dickie seemed like a real piece of work. You wouldn't want to get him mad.

"No, I guess not. How do I know it's good stuff? Where you got it stashed?"

"Oh, it's good stuff all right. I got it in a safe place. How much you gonna give me for it?"

"Seems like you're a might anxious to get rid of it. I'll give you twenty-five grand for it. But I'll have to test it first. Quality check, you know."

Brant thought about it for a minute. This guy would make three, or four, times as much. Mentally, he shook his head. This was no time to get greedy. At twenty-five thousand, he'd still come out ahead.

"Yeah, sure. I figured that. Okay, it's a deal. Where and when?"

"This is Monday? How about Wednesday night, here at midnight."

"Okay." Brant stood up, ready to leave. He had his hand on the doorknob when Dickie said, "I heard some dope got ripped off last night. This wouldn't be it now would it?"

"Uh, no, no, of course not." He quickly left the apartment.

CHAPTER FOUR

JESSIE PULLED IN the driveway. For a Tuesday it had been a remarkably busy day at the gas station. She sat for a few minutes, relaxing, then got out of the car and stretched her aching muscles. She pushed back her long, brown hair then reached back in the car and grabbed her purse and the account books she had brought with her.

As she opened the front door, Beany, her sister's cat, ducked outside, almost tripping her in the process. Jessie watched her run for her favorite spot in the yard, under Linda's rose bush. With a laugh, she set her books on the table in the entryway. It seemed very quiet in the house, unnaturally quiet. Jessie made her way through the house, cautiously peering in every room. On first glance, everything seemed normal. She shrugged off the feeling and grabbed a beer from the fridge, twisted off the cap and headed for the living room to relax.

She moved with a catlike grace. Her long legs seemed to glide across the room. As she walked, she reached up and lifted her shoulder-length hair off her neck, feeling the cooler air soothe her neck before she let it fall again.

Jessie sunk into a big, soft, comfortable chair and closed her eyes. Something wasn't right. Her eyes snapped open. Her lower jaw dropped. "What the heck . . . ?" She jolted upright in the chair.

"Linda? Linda? Where are you? I know you're here." Jessie couldn't believe her eyes. "Linda, damn you, where are you?" By this time, Jessie was out of the chair and moving purposefully toward the kitchen. Spying Linda outside, she headed out the back door, a full head of steam built up.

"Oh, hi, Jessie!" Linda stood there, hoe in hand and a small smile on her face. She looked at Jessie with cold blue eyes. "How was your day?" The insincerity was heavy in her voice.

"Don't play cute with me, Linda. Why? Why'd you do it? You know that plant was the last thing Mom gave me before she and Dad died." Jessie could feel the tears welling in her eyes.

Linda's face took on a falsely incredulous look. "Your plant? Which one? Last I looked they were all fine. Maybe Beany got into it." Linda turned away and went back to her hoeing.

"You know damn well what I'm talking about and don't go blaming this on Beany. This was you Linda, all you. Just own up to it, why don't you? Why?" Jessie didn't like the way she was starting to sound, like she was desperate. But she was feeling desperate. It wasn't the plant itself so much but what it represented.

"Well, well, what's the matter with little Ms. Perfect?" Linda spat the words out as she wheeled around and faced Jessie. "Losing your composure, are you? Or are you just acting like you always do?"

Jessie recoiled in surprise. This wasn't the Linda she knew. The Linda she knew was easygoing and friendly. Sure, they'd had their fights, but she had figured that was just sister rivalry. Linda was really worked up though. Her blonde hair was all over the place, her large body vibrating with emotion. Linda was always so careful about her appearance, believing that what she lacked in good looks she had to make up for in good grooming.

"What are you talking about?" Jessie took a step back. "Linda, what's going on?"

"You know, I've had it up to here" – Linda slashed across her forehead with her hand – "with you. Ever since you came to live with us, it's been 'Be careful with Jessie, she's had a hard time,' or 'Jessie doesn't know any better.' Well, I've had enough. Grow up! I wish" – by now her face was red with emotion – "I wish you had never come to live with us! I wish Mom and Dad had never adopted you. I wish I had never laid eyes on you!"

"I don't understand," Jessie managed to choke out, tears streaming down her face. "Why are you talking to me this way?"

"I decided to go through the rest of Mom's stuff, her personal stuff." Now it was Linda's turn for tears. "I, uh, I found something," she paused to catch her breath, the anger coming back again. "Something I'm sure I wasn't meant to find." She looked at Jessie with accusation-filled eyes. "She had written you a letter, she talked about how she was so happy to have you in our lives, how our family was now complete. Complete! As if we needed a snot-nosed brat like you around.

"She went on about you looking after Brant and me, as if we can't look after ourselves, like I'm some kind of a retard or something." By this time Linda was looking like a wild woman; tears were flying down her cheeks, spittle shooting from her mouth and her hair going every which way. "Just because I'm not as pretty as you or as slim as you or as popular. I always knew she loved you best, but I always hoped in my secret heart that it wasn't true. Well, now I have proof. I wish you would just get the hell out of my life. I don't ever want to see you again." She stalked past Jessie and slammed in to the house.

Jessie stood rooted to her spot, listening to Linda's anguished cries as she made her way upstairs, reeling from the verbal assault she had just received. After some time had passed she began to look around as though to reassure herself that the world was still the world, when she saw it.

It was a ball of paper, just lying there on the ground. Something anyone else would normally just ignore as garbage made Jessie walk over and pick it up. As she began to unroll the ball, she recognized her mother's handwriting. Her hands flew after that, smoothing out the paper, being careful not to tear it. It wasn't a letter at all, it was a page from Jill's diary and it had been written a few years before her death.

"Dear Diary," it read, "today was such a special day. We celebrated the tenth anniversary of Jessie's adoption. Just seeing the look on her face when she came downstairs this morning to see the kitchen all decorated was thanks enough for the last ten years.

"Jessie has grown to be such a beautiful girl. On the inside as well as the outside. I know she'll be able to take care of herself now, all the pain from the past put behind her.

"The only sad part of the day was when Linda shut herself in her room rather than take part in the special dinner we had tonight. I hope she can someday put aside this animosity she feels for Jessie.

"Brant was his usual outgoing self. He worships Jessie and it was so cute when he ran to be the first one to hug her this morning. It's so unusual for a boy his age to show emotion like that. He did turn red when he realized Bob and I were smiling at him for it.

"I am so thankful for today and every day. Our family is complete and I know that Jessie will look out for Linda and Brant if ever they should need her.

Thank you, God, for my husband and our three wonderful children."

Jessie wiped the tears from her cheeks as she was running in the house. She could hear crashing against the wall upstairs. Taking the steps two at a time, Jessie went to her room. Empty. Quickly, she checked Linda's room, no sign of her there either. Everything had gone quiet. Jessie finally found her in their parent's bedroom, sitting in a corner of the room, tears streaming down her cheeks.

"Linda!" Jessie cried, "What have you done?"

All of the ornaments, pictures and knickknacks had been taken off the dressers and thrown against the walls. Broken pieces of china and glass were strewn around the floor. The figurine Jessie gave them was in a hundred different pieces and ground into the carpet.

Jessie went to Linda and grabbed her by the shoulders. "What have you done?" she asked again while shaking her. "Your mother loved you! How could you destroy the keepsakes you have of her? That we have of her?" Jessie pushed away from her in exasperation and took a deep breath to attempt to calm herself. "Mom wasn't trying to put you down. That was her private journal and you took it completely out of context! Besides, it was written a long time ago."

Linda came up swinging. Jessie managed to block most of the blows but Linda had rage on her side; she was like a wild woman. She was screaming and swinging and backed Jessie up until she was in another corner. Jessie put her arms up over her face to try to deflect as many of the blows as possible but it was difficult. Linda was beyond reason, going for any opening she could find. She punched and kicked at Jessie's stomach and legs, causing Jessie to lose her breath.

Finally she'd had enough and started to fight back. She pushed back until Linda lost her balance and fell. "Enough!" Jessie screamed. "I've had it with your 'poor-little-me' act. You think Jill didn't love you? Well, tough. If you couldn't see how much she loved you, you're a poor excuse for a daughter. I envied you."

Linda's eyes widened with a look of incredulousness.

"Yes, envy. She may have felt sorry for me and came to love me, but you were her favorite. You want me out of here and out of your life? Well, fine. I'm outta here." Jessie turned to leave the room.

Linda picked herself up off the floor. "Good riddance," she spat after her. And not willing to leave well enough alone she added, "I may have been a poor excuse for a daughter but at least my mother wasn't a drunken drug addict."

Jessie thought she was beyond feeling any more pain, but all of a sudden, she was seven years old again, being told how useless she was. Back in her own room with the door closed, she gave in to the heartache she hadn't felt since her adopted Mom and Dad had died.

What was she going to do now? She gave in to the despair for a while, but soon, the tears dried up and her practical side once more asserted itself. She had started over once before when she was a child, she could certainly do it again now as an adult. But how? Where would she go?

Then it came to her.

Aunt Mae. Her biological father's widowed sister. There was something there, a bit of a memory and some information that was tucked away. Wait! Hiding place! It had been a very long time since Jessie had felt the need to access her secret box that held her special memories.

Jessie was very young the last time she saw Aunt Mae, probably three or four. She remembered because of how special the visit was and how hard she worked at remembering Aunt Mae just in case she needed her. When she was old enough, she wrote down her name. When she was adopted, Aunt Mae had written and Jessie had kept the letter and envelope.

Jessie got off her bed and got out her secret box. She went through her private papers and found the envelope. At the time, Aunt Mae had lived in Poplar Grove in British Columbia; Jessie hoped she still did. Maybe she could help Jessie feel like she really belonged somewhere.

At the bottom of the box, Jessie found the only picture she had saved from her childhood. It was a picture of a large house with a happy family posing in front. She had cut it out of a magazine and glued it to a piece of cardboard. The picture was faded now, but she still saw it as if it were new. She thought she had achieved that dream with the Lanes. That was all gone now. Jill and Bob were dead, the fight with Linda, that dream was over. She put the picture with the small pile of possessions she would take with her, including the page from Jill's diary.

There were a few things she would need to do, like quit her job and get some money. She still had her share of the life insurance money the Lanes had left them. She wouldn't be able to leave that night, but the next day, she would load up her car and head west to Poplar Grove.

CHAPTER FIVE

IT WAS WEDNESDAY afternoon before Jessie was finally on the road. With the sun overhead and the road stretched to infinity, she turned on the radio, already set to her favorite soft rock station, and cranked the volume.

Dan had hated to see her go; Jessie smiled to herself, replaying the scene in her mind. She'd been worried that he would be angry with her but in the end he had understood.

"You go, Jessie," he'd said. "I've felt for a long time that you needed to get away. 'Find yourself' as you young people are so fond of saying. Don't get me wrong though, I'm sorry to lose you, you've been the best bookkeeper I've had in a long, long time. But don't worry about me; I'll get along just fine. Doris will just have to come back to work for a while." Dan gave her a big hug. "If you decide to come back though, your job will be waiting for you."

He was such a nice man. If Jessie had a grandfather she'd want him to be just like Dan. Just thinking about that hug made Jessie smile again and feel warm all over. She had thought she'd be swallowed up whole; he was such a big teddy bear of a man.

Jessie braced her hands against the steering wheel and stretched. Her muscles were stiff and sore from Linda's vicious attack the night before. Physically, all she suffered were a few bruises; mentally, it was a different story. She shook it off.

Half an hour down the road, Jessie passed the turn off for Wayne's Junction. Every time she passed that sign, a cold shudder came over her and today was no different.

Jessie was born in Wayne's Junction on March 10, 1980, to Jim and Maureen Calden. Jim was a laborer who drank harder than he worked. Maureen wasn't much better by the time Jessie was four. Maureen had worked as a waitress at a local diner. For them, Jessie was an unwanted responsibility, since she interfered with party time.

By the time Jessie was six, she was on her own most of the time. Any attention Jim and Maureen paid her was offhand or abusive or both. Jessie took care of the household chores; she'd had to learn early how to survive.

Normal routine at the Calden house was Jim arriving home around eight or nine at night, already drunk. Maureen would get home by ten and then the arguing would start. One night, Maureen accused Jim of flirting with anything in a skirt or tight pants. She started slamming back whiskey. Jim yelled at Maureen that if she took better care of herself he wouldn't have to look around.

"If you were any kind of a man, I'd wanna look good for you," she'd slurred. "But who cares about a two-time loser like you?" By this time she'd had five or six shots of whiskey and she was just starting to warm up.

Jim knew that Maureen, drunk on whiskey and in a bad mood, was not good news for him. "Oh baby," he whined, "you know I does the best I can. It ain't my fault there's hardly any work out there. You know I work when I can, like now. Things would be a whole lot better if we didn't have that whiny brat hangin' around all the time. That was an accident that should've never happened."

"Jessie's okay," Maureen defended, "she looks after herself. Good thing too since I don't have any time for her. I didn't want her either but as long as she cleans up the place and stays out of our hair, there's not a lot we can do." Maureen walked across the kitchen and stumbled into a chair, her anger at Jim deflected into a shared misery. "Here, hon, have another drink."

Neither of them heard Jessie sob, as she made her way back to her room – not that it would have mattered. She had heard them arguing and got up to check on them. Just outside the kitchen door, Jessie had stopped and listened to everything. She'd been hearing it for as long as she could remember. She tried everything she knew to make her parents love her and be proud of her. Nothing she did ever made a difference. Jessie wasn't quite six years old.

The next two years were a nightmare for Jessie. The only relief she had was when she was at school. None of the other kids would play with her; they called her names and taunted her. Jessie was quiet and kept to herself. Her favorite subject was reading. She learned quickly, and she never took home any of the things she made at school since she knew they would only be laughed at.

At home, things steadily got worse. Her father was laid off again and would spend his time drinking. Her mother got hooked on drugs, cocaine mainly. Between the drugs and the alcohol, Maureen was getting meaner every day. By the time Jessie started the second grade, Maureen had been fired from her job as a waitress. Now both parents were at home all day. By the time Jessie came home from school, they were both either stoned or drunk or a combination of the two.

Jessie would normally go into the kitchen looking for a snack. Jim and Maureen would barely recognize that she was there. If it was a good day, Jessie would find some leftover tidbit of food then go outside. If it were a bad day then Jim or Maureen, or both, would poke and prod her until she started to cry.

"What's the matter with you?" they would taunt, "too sensitive? Make us something to eat!" they would then demand.

Jessie would look in the cupboards but it was usually futile. The only time there was food in the house was when there were leftovers from an all-nighter. She would search and search.

"I said, get us something to eat, you good-for-nothin' brat!" Maureen would yell at her. "I don't know why we keep you 'round here. You do nothin' but whine and cry. You don't even keep this pigsty clean anymore. Why don't you just get lost?" She would follow that up with a sharp slap across the face or some other part of Jessie's head if she managed to dodge fast enough.

As time went on Jessie was living in her mind more and more. In her imagination everything was beautiful. Maureen and Jim loved her; they pampered her and showered her with gifts. Sometimes Jessie would dream they were gone. She would grow up, be beautiful and everyone would want to know her.

Little did she know that one of her wishes would come true.

It was Jessie's eighth birthday. No one would remember and there wouldn't be a party or cake or presents. When Jessie came home from school expecting to find Jim and Maureen like she always did, drunk or stoned or both, she wasn't disappointed.

"What are you doing here?" Maureen demanded.

"School's over for today, Mommy," Jessie answered in a small voice.

"You know I hate it when you call me that! I hate any reminder that I'm a mother. Why don't you run out and play in the traffic?" she laughed. "You're good for nothing. You just cause me no end of aggravation. Get lost. I don't wanta see ya again tonight."

Jessie ran crying to her room. She threw herself down on her bed and sobbed. She knew it had been too much to hope they would remember her birthday but in her heart she had hoped things would be different today.

Eventually she stopped crying and rolled over until she slid down the side of her bed and landed on her knees. She clasped her hands together and leaned her elbows on her wrinkled blanket then bowed her head.

"Dear God," she prayed just like the Sunday school teacher had taught her. "I know I'm a bad girl and don't deserve anything, but it is my birthday and nobody else cares. I was thinking maybe you would. For my birthday I wish they were gone 'cause I hate them." She began crying again. "I'm sorry, God, I know I'm not s'posed to hate anybody, especially not my parents. Please, can I just have somebody to love me? I promise I'll be good."

With her prayer asked she climbed back on her bed and cried herself to sleep. When she woke up, it was dark and she was thirsty and had to use the bathroom. Being very careful to be quiet, she eased her bedroom door open and looked out.

All the lights in the house were on, but she couldn't hear Jim or Maureen. She went to the bathroom, and when she came out, she made her way to the kitchen, still being careful not to make any more noise than was absolutely necessary. Her parents didn't go to bed until the early morning hours so it was unusual for them not to be visible. Jessie shrugged but didn't think too much about it other than to feel relieved. She got her drink of water and decided to see if she could find them somewhere else in the house.

After cautiously searching every room, Jessie realized they weren't at home; they probably went out to get more booze or drugs or to meet with some of their friends. It had happened before. Jessie was just glad it was quiet; she went back to bed.

When she got up in the morning, they still weren't home so she got herself ready and went to school.

When she got home that afternoon, there still wasn't any sign of them. She decided to look around their bedroom; it was usually off-limits, but she decided it would be okay. Being extra quiet, just in case, Jessie eased open the door and found the room still empty. She walked in and looked around; the night before, she had only glanced in quickly enough to confirm that her parents weren't there. This time she felt braver and went right into the room. The bed was unmade and clothes were all over the floor and the closet was a mess. There were a few clothes there but she could see that Maureen's favorite shirt was missing. She took a closer look through the laundry littering the floor and still couldn't find it. Jessie began to hope.

On her way to the kitchen, she stopped in the living room; it was as empty as always. Jessie remembered when they used to have a television and a stereo but they were long gone, sold for money to buy drugs.

In the kitchen, Jessie started searching for food and was pleased when she came up with some leftover pizza, which must have been from the night before. That day, all she'd had to eat was the free lunch the school provided. Within minutes, she had eaten two large pieces and then, not sure what to do, she cleaned the kitchen. By the time she was finished, it was late and she was exhausted.

There was still no sign of her parents, so she went to bed.

CHAPTER SIX

THREE DAYS WENT by and still there was no sign of her parents. As each day went by Jessie began to relax a little more. She began to smile a little more often and to participate in class. One of her teachers noticed the changes and wondered what had happened.

"Has anyone noticed a difference in little Jessie Calden?" Jill Lane asked the other teachers in the staff lunchroom.

"I have," one of them answered. "She seems a little friendlier and happier. I wonder what has happened?"

"Does anyone know her parents?" Jill asked.

"I don't know them but I've heard about them," yet another teacher answered. "I hear that they are heavily into drugs and alcohol. That poor kid."

"I'm going to see what I can find out." Jill left the room in search of Jessie. She found her in the classroom.

"Hi Jessie. Can I speak with you for a moment?"

Jessie looked up and smiled. "Okay." Jill walked her away from the other children so they could speak privately.

Jill knelt down to be at eye level with Jessie. "Jessie, is everything okay at home? Has anything happened or changed?"

"Why do you ask?" Jessie really liked Mrs. Lane but teachers asking questions, especially about home, was never a good thing. Besides she didn't want to tell anyone about her parents.

"Well," Jill wanted to be honest with Jessie but didn't want to scare her either. "You seem different the last couple of days. I just wondered what happened to change things. I don't think I've seen you smile so much. It's nice to see, it lights up your face. Has something wonderful happened? Can you tell me about it?"

Jessie was fighting the urge to tell Mrs. Lane about her good luck because she didn't want anyone to find her parents. As long as she could eat at school, everything would be fine.

"Not really, Mrs. Lane. My mommy made me promise not to tell." Jessie stared at the floor and slid her right foot back and forth. She stole a quick glance at Mrs. Lane to see if she believed her or not.

Jill could see that Jessie wasn't telling her everything. "Well, okay, Jessie, I wouldn't want you to break a promise. You would tell me if you needed help with anything, wouldn't you?"

"Yes, Mrs. Lane." Jessie struggled not to tell her favorite teacher everything and bit her tongue to help her keep the smile from her face. She continued to fight the urge to tell.

Jill finally left the room although her instincts were telling her to stay and keep talking to Jessie. Something wasn't quite right here but badgering a little girl wasn't the way to go about figuring out what was going on. She would do some checking around, go and talk to the parents just to be sure everything was okay. There was such a radical change in Jessie, there had to be a reason and she needed to find out what it was.

Once school was over for the day, Jill followed Jessie home being careful not to let Jessie see her. She needn't have worried; Jessie never once looked back. That confirmed one thing for Jill, that Jessie wasn't afraid of anything. When Jessie entered the dilapidated house Jill felt sorry for her but it seemed safe so Jill headed back to the school to get her car. Now that she knew where Jessie lived, she would drop in on the parents the next day.

The next morning Jill had a free hour and decided that was as good a time as any to pay a visit to the Calden home. She parked on the street and walked to the front door. She knocked three times with no response and waited a few extra minutes before she gave up and wandered around the back of the house, looking in the windows as she went. It seemed like no one was home; she'd have to try later.

Toward the end of the school day, Jill asked one of the other teachers to keep Jessie after school for half an hour to give her a chance to speak with Jessie's parents.

As she went back to the Calden house, Jill wondered just what she would say to Jessie's parents. Would they be approachable? Just how do you ask someone why his or her daughter is all of a sudden happy?

This time she pulled her car into the driveway. Again there was no answer at the door. It seemed strange to her that no one was home, especially when school was out for the day.

On her way home, she picked up Brant from daycare, distracted, thinking about Jessie, determined to figure out what was going on.

"Linda, do you know Jessie Calden?" she asked her daughter when they got home.

"Mom, she's in second grade and I'm in fourth. Why would I know her?"

"Okay, do you know anything about her or her parents? From the other kids?"

"I heard her Mom and Dad are druggies and drunks," she giggled. "Druggies, what is that Mom? Anyway, all the kids pick on her. Why do you want to know?"

"Oh, I'm just trying to get in touch with them."

"She's just a loser," Linda shrugged, "who cares?"

"Linda! She is not a loser! I'll not have you talking about anyone like that, do you hear me?"

"Yes, Mom." Linda beat a hasty retreat to her room.

Jill's husband, Bob, got home from work at dinnertime. After the meal was finished, Jill pulled him in to the kitchen. "Honey, do you know Jim or Maureen Calden?"

"There's a bad news pair if I've ever heard of one," he responded. Bob worked as a guard at the local jail. "I hear they're both substance abusers, both unemployed and living on welfare. They have a little girl, poor thing. Something weird is going on with them. There's a rumor going around the station that they are in debt to some drug dealer. Supposedly they've skipped town. Why do you ask?"

"Their daughter, Jessie, is in my class. She's been acting differently the last few days. When I asked her about it, she said her mother made her promise not to say, but something didn't seem quite right about that. She couldn't really look me in the eye, and that's very unusual for Jessie."

"Acting differently how?" Bob asked.

"She's seemed much happier," Jill responded. "She's been smiling more often, participating in class. I wouldn't normally question that type of behavior, but since she joined my class, she's been very quiet and shy."

"Well," Bob responded, "I would be happy too if my parents were like that and just disappeared. She probably has no idea what happened to them. Maybe she just feels relief."

"She's such a pretty girl; she has wavy brown hair, and she's a little on the thin side, but with addicted parents I guess that's not much of a surprise. Bob, she's all alone and I'd like to help her. What do you think?"

Bob looked at Jill with eyes narrowed. "What kind of help are you talking about?"

"We could take her in, Bob. I know it sounds like a lot," she rushed to add when she saw the question in his eyes. "No, I haven't given it a lot of thought, it just came to me. The poor little thing probably hasn't been shown any real love and we have a big house and lots of love." She looked at him with all of her love shining through her eyes, "What do you think?"

"I know you when you get on a crusade," he replied, shaking his head, "I don't stand a chance. It's not necessarily a bad idea, but what about Linda and Brant? They have to be in on this as well since this will affect them too. Are you sure you know what you're getting us into? If this child has been neglected or abused, she could have emotional and behavioral problems. Do you think we're ready and able to cope with that?"

Jill's eyes were bright with unshed tears. "Oh, Bob, I hadn't thought of neglect or abuse. That poor child. You are right though; we'll have to discuss this as a family. I do want to bring her here to us. She's such a sweet child. I know we can help her."

Bob thought for a few moments. "Doesn't this sort of thing take forever? I mean, whenever I've heard someone talk about adoption, they complain about how long it takes. Have you thought about that?"

"No, I hadn't." Jill began pacing. "There has to be some way around that issue. Besides, we aren't talking about adoption." She stopped pacing and looked at Bob. "Are we?"

"What else is there?"

"There has to be some sort of emergency shelter or something for kids in trouble, something like foster care. Maybe we could do that. I'll have to check it out, but in the meantime, let's talk to the kids and see what they think."

They assembled Linda and Brant in the kitchen and sat them at the breakfast bar. Jill took the lead and explained what they wanted to do.

Linda was the first to voice an opinion: "No way!" she exclaimed. "She's a dirty little grubber and she'll want to play with all my stuff. Besides, she'll just get in the way. No way in the world!"

"Linda!" Bob admonished. "That's no way to talk about anyone. We have a lot and Jessie has nothing. It wouldn't hurt for us to share. Now, do you have anything else to say?"

"I'm sorry, Daddy, it's just that I like things the way they are and I don't want it to change. But I guess it would be all right just for a little while." Linda adored her father and didn't like it when he was upset with her.

"Thank you, Linda," Jill responded. "Brant, what about you?"

"I don't care, I s'pose it would be okay. Couldn't you find a boy instead though? Somebody for me to play with?"

Brant was four years old. He had been hinting that he would like a playmate ever since one of his friends had gotten a new baby brother, and he thought that was so neat that he should have one too.

"So we are all in agreement then?" Jill looked at Bob for confirmation.

"I guess it does, honey. I don't know how you do that – get me to agree to things without my even realizing it!" Bob put his arms around Jill and kissed her on the lips.

"Yuck!" Brant and Linda cried out together.

"What about tonight though? What if she's in danger?"

"She's been okay these last few days and until we know for sure what's happened, we don't want to go barging in. Do you remember what happened the last time we thought a child needed rescuing?"

Jill's eyes opened wide and a small gasp escaped her lips. "Oh yes, right," she replied. "We don't want a repeat."

A few years earlier, when Brant was just a baby, there had been rumors of child abuse involving a neighbor just down the street. Jill had talked Bob into removing the child without notifying anyone or even making sure there was a problem. They ended up being charged with kidnapping although the charge was later dropped. It turned out there had been abuse, but it involved the babysitter and not the parents.

The next day, Jill called Social Services and inquired about taking a child into their home without saying who it was. They'd have to get all the information they could before they proceeded. It just couldn't take very long, that's all. Bob was checking with the officers at the station and they got together for lunch to compare notes.

"What did you find out?" Jill asked Bob.

"They've definitely done a runner. Sam was talking to one of his snitches and he said they were seen leaving town. What did you get from Social Services?"

"They wouldn't say a lot without knowing who we were talking about, but I did find out that if a child has to be removed from the home, they get sent to a foster home. The person I talked to wasn't going to say any more without some details. I told him there was a little girl I knew who would need a good home and that we wanted to take her in. He told me we would have to be approved before we could act as a foster home. I told him we didn't have a lot of time. He said in an emergency, they have a shortcut way to approve people. He tried to get more from me, but I stalled and said I would contact him later."

Jill leaned across the table and took Bob's hand in hers. "Bob, we have to do this. It's the right thing. I feel it in my heart."

Bob looked at Jill with a smile. "You know, this is why I fell in love with you; you are so good to everyone around you. I've been thinking about this all day. You know, going over the pros and cons. From everything you've told me, it feels right to me too, and I don't even know Jessie."

Jill's eyes lit up and a smile filled her face. "Okay, let's do it. I'll talk to Jessie. Then I'll call Social Services again. I'd like her to be with us tonight, if possible. I don't want her to be alone another night."

They left the restaurant. Once outside, they quickly hugged and went their separate ways.

When Jill got back to the school she decided to talk to the principal first. He needed to know what was going on.

She walked up to the secretary's desk. "Is he in?"

"Yes, he is, but I don't know if he's seeing anyone right now. Hold on a minute while I check." Marj turned away and pushed a button on the telephone. "Mr. Taylor, Mrs. Lane is here to see you." Marj listened for a moment and then nodded. "You can go right in."

"Thanks, Marj." Jill knocked once before she walked in to the office.

Mr. Taylor was on the phone and waved at Jill to take a seat on the chair opposite him. "Okay, Mary, I'll remember," he said into the phone, then hung up.

"I can't figure her out sometimes," he chuckled. "This is the third time she's called to remind me about the baby's pictures. Is she a proud mother or what?"

"Everyone's like that, especially with the first one. You can admit it to me, you're as proud as punch yourself, aren't you?" Jill smiled.

He leaned forward as though he was about to tell a secret. "Don't tell Mary, but yes, I am. Anyway, you didn't want to see me so I could bore you about the baby. What can I do for you?"

Jill took a deep breath to steady her nerves. "I'm here about Jessie Calden." She then told him everything she knew. When she was finished, he had a grim look on his face.

"I was aware that there were problems," Taylor sat back in his chair as he digested the information Jill had just given him. "That was one of the reasons we switched Jessie to your class. I didn't tell you the whole reason because I didn't want to influence you in any way. I suppose we'll have to contact Social Services." He reached for the phone.

"Wait," Jill rushed in and pushed the disconnect button. "There's more."

Taylor put the phone down slowly while looking at Jill for an explanation.

"Bob and I want to take her in," Jill quickly added. "I'll square it with Social Services since I've already been in contact with them. The guy I spoke to said that in an emergency he could qualify us as a temporary foster home."

"Are you sure about this Jill? Granted, Jessie is a sweet little girl, but she does have more than her share of problems. Do you think you can handle that?"

"I've discussed this with Bob, and we both agree that we'd like to give it a try as long as Social Services give us the go-ahead."

Taylor leaned back in his chair, steepled his hands together, and thought for a few moments. Finally, "Yes, I think you would do well with her. If you need a reference give them my name. I hope it all works out for you, Jill."

Jill was relieved; the first hurdle was crossed. "I hope it does too; thanks for your support. I'll let you know what Social Services has to say."

Back in the staff room, Jill called the social worker again, only this time, she told him everything. He agreed that speed was the key in this situation. Jill answered all of his questions and was told he would get back to her later that day.

"Have you said anything to Jessie about any of this?" he asked.

"No, not yet," she replied. "I thought I'd wait until I heard from you. I'm not sure how she's going to take this. It would be better if I talked to her after school."

The social worker agreed and once again said he would be in touch as soon as he could.

After Jill hung up the phone, she sat staring at the wall for a while, questioning what they were doing. Was it the right thing? But the thought of Jessie on her own quickly changed her mind. Jill got up and headed for class.

The call came in just before three o'clock.

Everything was set and now Jill was nervous. She caught up with Jessie just as school was letting out for the day.

"Jessie!" she called out.

Jessie turned and walked back to Jill, her face scrunched up with worry. After all, Mrs. Lane is a teacher, and you only get called back if you're in trouble.

"Jessie, I need to talk to you. Come with me." Jill led her to an empty classroom.

Jessie looked around with wild eyes. "What have I done, Mrs. Lane? I was good today. Wasn't I? Am I in trouble?"

"No, Jessie, you're not in trouble," Jill was quick to try to reassure her, but she could see Jessie was skeptical. "You were a good girl today." Jill's eyes were watering with unshed tears. This poor little girl feels so bad about herself . . . she took a deep breath.

"Jessie, I know your mom and dad are gone."

"What do you mean?" Jessie looked wary. "They're not gone. They just went to, uh, Brady. They'll be back."

"No, Jessie. They are gone." Jill spoke softly. "They're gone and it looks like they won't be back."

Jessie couldn't hold back her tears any longer. "It's all my fault," she cried. "If I wasn't such a bad girl, such a burden, they wouldn't be gone. Now no one will want me."

Jill felt her heart break for Jessie as she gathered her in her arms and held her tight. "No, Jessie, you're not a bad girl, you're not a burden." Silent anger filled her. Jessie was too young to know the word "burden," let alone what it meant. Jill held the sobbing girl in her arms.

"There, there, Jessie, I'm here for you," Jill said over and over. "I'm going to take care of you. I want you, Jessie. We'll go to your house and get some of your things and then you'll come home with me and be part of my family. Do you think that might be okay?"

Jessie had slowly grown quiet. Finally she asked, "Really?"

"Yes, Jessie, really. You'll have to share a room with my daughter Linda though; do you think you might like that?"

"Yes, I'd like that." Jessie looked both hopeful and wary. "Are you sure it's okay? I can be a handful, you know."

"I'm sure it's okay," Jill laughed. "You'll be just fine."

Jessie's new life had started. It wasn't always easy. It took a long time before she felt safe. Linda didn't like her and Brant idolized her. With a lot of adjustment, Jessie finally fit in.

When Jessie was ten years old, the Lanes adopted her. It was the happiest day of her life. She finally felt part of a real family.

Until now, that is.

CHAPTER SEVEN

B RANT WALKED IN the front door. "Hello!" he yelled. "I'm home!" A noise in the kitchen caught his attention, so he went there to investigate.

"Hey, Linda, something sure smells good in here." Brant lifted the lid off the pot and smelled the contents. "Where's Jessie?"

"Get away from there!" She slapped his hand away from the stir spoon. "You'll just have to wait until supper."

Brant stuck out his lower lip and tried to look soulfully at his sister. "Aw, sis, just a little taste? Please?" he implored.

"No, you brat," she smiled at him. The fact that she smiled should have told him something was different. "Go wash up. Supper will be ready in ten minutes." Linda kept stirring the sauce; the smile didn't quite leave her face but the reason for it had now changed.

"Oh, all right, party pooper. Where's Jessie?" he asked again but he was already leaving the room and failed to notice Linda stiffen when he mentioned Jessie's name again.

When Brant didn't get an answer as he had expected to, he turned back, finally sensing that something wasn't quite right. Linda was arranging garlic bread pieces on a pan but he noticed her right hand was shaking slightly.

"Linda, what's going on?" he asked her, finally really looking at her face.

"Nothing. I'm busy. Go wash for supper." She steadfastly refused to look at him, making sure to keep her face out of his view.

Brant didn't know what was going on but he knew he couldn't overreact, just in case he tipped Linda off to what he had done. He backed away and quickly went to the bathroom to clean up and take a few minutes to think and try to make some sense of what was going on. While he was washing his hands he realized that any time Linda was in a "mood," she and Jessie had had a major blowout. Even though he had been wrapped up in his own mess the last couple of days, he realized he hadn't seen or talked to Jessie in that time. Not that he could say that was unusual, what with his nocturnal wanderings and trying to stay hidden from Stack.

On the other hand, he hadn't seen Jessie's car in the driveway either. She was usually home before him, even when he came home straight after work.

He shivered. Tonight was the big night. Just thinking about it was giving him the willies. Jessie *had* to be home before midnight, she just had to be. But what if she wasn't?

Brant realized he'd been drying his hands so hard they were red from the friction. Agitated now, he rushed back to the kitchen to confront Linda.

"Where's Jessie?" he demanded.

Linda looked him in the eyes. "I don't know," she told him, "and I don't care."

"What do you mean, you don't know and you don't care? What's going on?" Brant's eyes were wide with alarm and beads of sweat began to shine on his forehead. "Linda?" His voice got louder. "Linda? What the hell is going on? Where is she? Where's Jessie?" By the time he finished speaking, his face was only a few centimeters from hers.

Tears of fear began to gather at the corners of Linda's eyes. "I don't know, Brant." Her face turned red and a wild look came to her eyes. "I don't know," she repeated. "How many times do I have to say it?" By then she was breathing hard and shouting herself. "I hope she never comes back!"

Like flipping a switch off, she turned and began dishing up dinner as if nothing had happened. Her slightly jerky movements betrayed her though since she could hardly see what she was doing. Brant grabbed the pot away from her and slammed it back down on the stove.

"Would you please tell me what is going on? Did you two have another fight? Did she go to Sally's place?" Brant started to calm down slightly. Yes, that was it; she must have gone to Sally's. "Well, did she?"

"How the hell should I know?" She turned to face Brant. "And why do you care so much anyway? Do you need money again? Is that it? Poor Brant always needs his idol to bail him out. Well, it won't happen this time, brother." Linda's eyes went steel-hard. A little smile played at the corner of her mouth. The calmer she was, the more fearful Brant was.

"Just tell me what happened, Linda."

Slowly, Linda finished dishing up the sauce and spaghetti. She pulled the garlic bread from the oven and arranged it in the basket.

Brant was beside himself with anxiety; something big was going on.

Finally, "we had a fight."

"So what else is new," Brant shrugged, trying but failing to be nonchalant.

"So this was a big one," she responded. "I was going through some of Mom's stuff yesterday, since I figured it was time." Linda carefully walked each dish to the table; very deliberately setting them down as though each had to be placed in precisely the correct manner. "Anyway, I found something. I found Mom's journal." Her voice began to crack, her words coming out a little faster.

"I read some of it, I know I shouldn't have, but I just couldn't help it. I miss her and Dad so much. Anyway, I opened it to a page where Mom was writing about Jessie and us and I just saw red . . ."

"Linda, slow down," Brant broke in, "I can't understand what you're saying." He put his hand on her arm to stop her automatic movements between the stove and the table. She walked back to the table and sat down. Brant followed and sat across from her.

Linda took a deep breath so she could continue. "I read it, Mom's diary entry. It was written quite some time ago. In it Mom says how much she loves Jessie, how she made our family complete. Complete! Can you believe it? Anyway, immediately I saw red." By this time Linda was wringing her hands, unknowingly shredding a paper napkin to pieces. "I was so upset I wanted to lash out and it didn't matter to who or what. I went to the living room and tore up the plant Mom gave Jessie just before they died." Then she smiled, remembering, one of those small, secret, evil little smiles. "It felt so good and I knew it would hurt Jessie." Her gaze fixed on the far wall and she was lost in reliving the memory.

Brant snapped his fingers in front of her face to bring her back. "There's more, Linda, isn't there? What else have you done?" The dread was like a dead weight in his gut.

Linda reluctantly and slowly turned her head to Brant. "Yes, there is more." She spoke in a low steady tone and Brant felt the shivers move up and down his spine. He fought not to think the worst.

"Tell me," he demanded. "All of it."

"I tore up her plant, like I said, and it felt really good and then I calmed down a little. I figured I would go and work in the garden until Jessie got home; let her find the mess I had made." Again she smiled that secret smile. "I was hilling the potatoes when Jessie came tearing out of the house yelling for me. We got into an argument and I told her about the diary. Then I told her I hated her, that I wanted her out of our lives.

"After that I went running to the house, I was still so upset and mad. I ran up to Mom and Dad's room and just started throwing things. In my rage I didn't know what I was doing. I saw a figurine Jessie had given them and it hit me all over again. I smashed it against the floor and ground the pieces into the carpet." Tears of self-pity and anger were trickling down her cheeks.

Brant wanted to comfort her but just couldn't find it within himself to do it; he was too worried about himself. He prodded her to continue.

"I sat in the corner of their room, hugging myself and crying. Jessie came into the room and started yelling at me, at the destruction I had caused. She shook me and that got me going again. I flew into another rage, hitting her over and over. She finally started to fight back and knocked me down. She said if I wanted her gone that badly she'd go. She left this morning and I haven't seen her since." She took in a deep, shuddering breath, "Good riddance," she added.

Everything she had said hit him all at once.

"Oh my god, Linda. Do you have any idea what you have done?" By the time he spoke the last word, Brant was yelling at Linda, the panic vivid in his face. "Do you have any idea? You are such a selfish bitch!"

"How dare you!" Linda screamed back at him. "She stole just as much from you."

"What the hell are you talking about? Jessie never stole anything in her life. Not from me, you or anyone else." By this time, Brant was pacing back and forth, trying to figure out what he was going to do now.

"Mom and Dad, you nitwit. The love we should have gotten was squandered on that, that hag! Everything she got should have been ours, not hers!"

"Linda, I can't believe you." He'd been hearing versions of this for as long as he could remember. He didn't have time for this now but he had to say something to shut her up. "Mom and Dad loved us; all three of us. We didn't lose out on anything. You've been so busy hating Jessie that you never took advantage of what we had. I feel sorry for you. Now, thanks to you, I'm a dead man and you're a selfish lonely bitter person."

Linda sprang from her chair so fast Brant never knew what hit him. She pushed him hard enough to slam him against the wall, knocking down a picture in the process. The sound of breaking glass was barely audible over the sound of their breathing.

"What was that for?" he asked, shaking his head to clear it.

"You feel sorry for me?" Linda screamed, little pieces of spit flying out of her mouth. "I can't believe you don't see what that conniving bitch cost us!"

"I've had enough!" he yelled back at her. "That's all you do, moan and complain about Jessie. She's been good to me, I love her, and she's my sister. You're so wrapped up in your hatred you don't care what happens to anyone else. I tell you, if Jessie really has left town I'm a dead man."

"You're serious?" Linda finally heard his words.

"Damn right I am." Brant resumed his pacing. "I am so dead. What am I gonna do now? Oh my god, oh my god." He was smoothing his hair back so much it was plastered to his head; his eyes were wide and wild, his head bobbing up and down, up and down.

"Brant, stop." Linda put her hand out to slow him down. "Tell me what's going on, what have you done? Does this have something to do with why you got beat up?"

"I can't tell you, I've got to get out of here, figure this out by myself." He raced to the front door, grabbed his car keys and slammed out the door.

He sat in his car for a long time, hugging the steering wheel. The more he thought about things, the more scared he became. What could he do now? Dickie he might be able to stall, but Stack? He'd promised him the money by Thursday and it was already Wednesday. What was he going to do?

He'd have to find Jessie.

Figuring that he had some sort of plan, he started the car. He would check all of Jessie's normal hangout spots and talk to her friends. Someone would know where she was.

Two hours later he pulled in the parking lot of an abandoned warehouse. Jessie was nowhere to be found, and no one had seen or heard from her. He still had three hours before he was due at Dickie's place. Something would come to him in the meantime; it just had to.

CHAPTER EIGHT

B RANT WAS FRANTIC. He had managed to stall Dickie by using a lame excuse about being called in to work. How he had pulled it off Brant wasn't sure but he wasn't going to question it too closely. Dickie insisted that he had to have the delivery by noon on Thursday and he only had two hours left.

He hadn't slept at all. Over and over through the night, all he could do was try to figure out how to find Jessie. It wasn't until seven that morning that he remembered Dan, her boss. He was so relieved he was halfway into his car before something made him stop and think a little. Maybe it was a bit early for Dan to be at work, maybe he should wait a bit, and maybe he should try to calm down. He had caught a glimpse of himself in the side-view mirror on his car and almost scared himself. He decided to buy some time and go in the house and take a shower, clean up a bit, try and slow his heart rate down.

When Brant arrived at the station, Dan was there, just unlocking the door. Brant immediately began asking questions about Jessie, but Dan wasn't saying much. Brant was getting frustrated. Finally, Dan told him that all he knew was that Jessie had had enough of Linda's bull and had taken off for parts unknown.

"Oh, come on, Dan! I'm sure she told you more than that! I need to know where she is. Please, please tell me!" Brant pleaded. Dan shook his head and shrugged his shoulders as if to say he'd already said all he knew.

"You're full of shit, Dan, I know it and you know it! I can't do this. If I don't find Jessie in the next," he quickly glanced at his watch, "in the next three hours, I might as well just go kill myself!"

"Brant, I've heard it all before. What do you expect from Jessie? From me? Look at you, all wild and out of control. I'm telling you the truth, all I know is she had to get away. She may have said something about heading west but that's all I know." As soon as the words were out of his mouth, Dan knew he had given too much away. Damn!

"West? Why west? It doesn't much matter now, does it? I'm dead anyway."

An hour later he was still sitting in his car trying to decide what to do next. His mind was blank and every time he tried to think, his head hurt. He decided he'd better find Dickie and tell him what happened. He started the car and pulled away from the curb.

They were scheduled to meet at noon but Brant decided to take a chance that Dickie would be there even though it was early. He took his time driving, working on a plan. It seemed to take hardly any time at all and he found himself on the staircase climbing up to Dickie's apartment. Each step was slower and his legs felt heavier. Before he was ready he had reached the door on the fourth floor.

Breathing in deeply through his mouth so he didn't have to smell that smell any more than necessary, he knocked on the door.

No one answered.

He knocked again, only this time a little louder. He quickly looked over his shoulders to see if anyone from the neighboring apartments was going to stick their heads out and yell at him, but so far the coast was clear. He finally heard someone moving around inside the apartment.

"Who is it?" a female voice called out.

"Um, it's, uh Brant. Brant Lane. Is Dickie there?"

"Just a sec," was the reply.

Brant waited in the hallway. He had no choice but to look around and what he saw didn't help his nervous stomach. The carpet looked like it used to be plush at one time but was threadbare or caked with garbage or other substances that gave off a rankly rotten odor. He had almost worked up the courage to kick apart one particularly colorful mound when the apartment door swung open.

There stood Dickie with a cigarette hanging out of the side of his mouth, the smoke causing him to squint his left eye. "This better be good," he growled.

"Sorry 'bout this Dickie, but you'll want to hear it." Brant wiped his sweat-covered hands on the back of his jeans. "Can I come in?" He glanced both ways down the long hallway.

"Yeah, ya better. Don't sit down though, ya won't be stayin' long." He closed the door behind him.

Brant walked into the living room area of the apartment, not sure where to stand, so he wandered back and forth in front of the couch.

"Well, spit it out," Dickie demanded. "You better not be here to give me bad news." Dickie plopped himself into his chair causing a large cloud of dust to rise into the air.

"I don't know how to say this." Brant walked back and forth in front of the couch, stealing glances at Dickie to gauge the reaction as the story unfolded.

"Something terrible has happened." It wasn't looking good already. Dickie's eye's had already narrowed and his expression was grimmer than usual.

"Oh?" Just one innocent word but the way Dickie said it made Brant very afraid.

"Uh, yeah. It's about the coke." Brant was still pacing and glancing, wiping his hands every few seconds.

"Spit it out," Dickie demanded. "I ain't got all damn day. I got a feelin' I ain't gonna like this." The snarl was back.

Brant kept his eyes on the grimy carpet. He stopped pacing, his hands now in his pockets and he took as deep a breath as he dared. The words came out in a rush. "I stashed the stuff in my sister's car. When I got home yesterday I found out she'd had a big fight with my other sister and then she took off. I've searched everywhere but I can't find her. This morning I checked with her boss. He said she'd quit her job, said she was leaving town." He finally stole a quick glance at Dickie. "Oh man, am I in deep shit."

Dickie jumped out of his chair. Brant never thought such a large man could move that fast. He rushed at Brant, swinging his meaty fist. Brant caught the blow on his left cheek; his head snapped around, spit and blood flying out of his mouth.

"You little cocksucker!" Dickie screamed. "You're trying to rip me off!" His face was beet-red, a vein in his forehead throbbed. "Goddamn you, Lane. What the fuck do you expect me to do about it?"

Brant was still on the floor where he had fallen, tears running down his face but whether they were from pain or self-pity was anyone's guess. He took a deep, trembling breath.

"I, I don't know," he managed to whine. "Help me get it back? Stall Stack for me?"

"Stall Stack? What the hell are you talking about?"

Too late, Brant realized he'd said too much. He shook his head saying, "Nothing, nothing. I, uh, I just figured you'd be selling it to him. Yeah." He cringed, expecting to feel another meaty smack from Dickie.

Dickie went into the kitchen and grabbed a beer. "Delores!" he yelled. "Get your ass in here and cook me some breakfast. I've got to think."

Delores came out of the bedroom and went straight to the kitchen. She pulled out the only clean pan she could find and, as quietly as possible, she broke three eggs into it and stirred them with an old, dirty fork.

Dickie went back to the living room and looked at Brant with disgust. "Quit sniveling, you little bastard. And get your ass up off the floor. Sit down on the couch."

Brant quickly responded, holding his throbbing cheek. The inside of his mouth had stopped bleeding but it was throbbing. The bruises from the end of the previous week were beginning to fade, but now he'd have new ones. He swiped at his nose with the sleeve of his shirt, then sat on the couch.

By this time, Dickie had calmed down slightly. "Now, tell me everything, don't leave nothin' out," he demanded.

Brant went through the whole story right from the beginning. He was talking about his visit with Dan that morning when it hit him. "Dan said something about where she'd gone. Well, not where . . ." he snapped his fingers trying to remember. "No, that's it! He said she'd headed west!"

Delores brought out the plate of food. Dickie grabbed it out of her hand and told her, "Now get back in the bedroom where you belong." He got to work shoveling food in his mouth. Brant felt sick to his stomach just listening to him, let alone seeing it. He leaned back on the couch, waiting.

It didn't take long. Dickie cleaned off the plate, let out a belch and dropped the plate on the floor near his feet. "I gotta make a call," was all he said before he heaved himself out of the chair and went to the kitchen.

Brant tried to listen in to the conversation, but couldn't make out anything. So he sat there waiting, feeling nothing but resignation. He'd really done it this time. It had seemed so easy Monday night, but just his luck, almost in the clear again and wham! Something happens. He closed his eyes. If only . . . Yeah, the story of his life.

Dickie finally came back in the room. Brant opened his eyes.

"Okay," Dickie announced, "we're going for a ride." He grabbed his coat and headed for the door.

"Where are we going?"

"You'll see. Let's go."

The fear was back again as a big empty hollow in his gut.

He followed Dickie's instructions and pulled in to the industrial area, to a storage facility. Dickie told him where to stop. He turned off the car and they sat there waiting.

Finally Brant asked what they were doing there.

"Just shut up," came the reply. "We're waiting for someone."

Fifteen long minutes later, Brant finally saw a car pulling in behind them. He thought he recognized it in the rearview mirror; he spun around in his seat.

"Holy shit!" he exclaimed. "That's Stack!" Beads of sweat popped out on his forehead. He swung back to Dickie. "What is this? Are you trying to get me killed?"

"You should have been straight with me. Shut up and get out of the car."

Brant didn't know what to think. Were they going to shoot him now? He got out of the car, looking between Dickie and the other car, over and over. Should he make a run for it? No, they'd run him over. Maybe if he waited to find out for sure what was going to happen, he might be able to figure a way out.

Dickie walked around to the front of Brant's car. He came up behind Brant and shoved him toward Stack's car. Brant stumbled forward a few steps then walked toward the car with Dickie behind him. When they were abreast of the driver's door, the back door opened and Stack stepped out. For such a little man he made Brant very nervous. Brant stopped where he was and Dickie came around beside him.

"Well, well, well. What have we here?" Stack reached out and touched Brant's face. "Got smacked around a bit, did you? Couple times by the look of you."

Brant watched him warily. What was going to happen now?

"Dickie has told me a very interesting story." Stack looked Brant over from head to toe. "Do you know the story he told me?"

Brant looked at Dickie then back at Stack. Realization came slowly.

"That's right, pea brain. Dickie here works for me. Didn't know that? Not very smart of you." Stack shook his head. "Tsk, tsk, tsk. What I can't figure out is why you thought you'd get away with your little stunt. You're just lucky you didn't take it all, otherwise we wouldn't be having this conversation. You'd already be polluting one of the lakes around here." He laughed, and Dickie joined in. "I gotta give you some credit though. It's not every day I get someone with the balls to steal dope from me and then turn around and try to sell it back to me. To pay back money owed to me."

Before Brant could catch his breath, Stack slapped his right cheek.

"You little prick," he snarled. "I still ought to kill you and I just might, later. First though, we need to get that coke back. It sounds like we're gonna need to take a little trip." He turned to Dickie. "Stash his car in storage," he ordered. "You" – he pointed to Brant – "get your ass in the back of the car."

Brant just stood there, mouth hanging open, unable to respond. Stack grabbed his arm and pushed him into the car. "Don't try anything cute," he warned. "Mike there has a gun. You run or do anything else stupid and he'll shoot to kill, it's that simple. You got it?"

Brant picked himself off the backseat, glanced at the driver who flashed the gun, and nodded. He pushed himself into the corner of the seat against the door. Stack got in beside him. They followed Dickie driving Brant's car. Once that car was hidden away, Dickie got in the front with Mike.

"Head west," Stack ordered.

Tim Stack was a small-town, big-time crook. When he was a teenager, he had gotten in trouble by taking bets from his peers and when they didn't pay he beat them up. He came to the attention of the RCMP when he went too far once, almost killing one of his customers. The boy's parents had complained and Tim had been charged with assault with intent. He was found guilty and spent six months in a youth facility.

It was the best education he had ever received. When he was released he found someone else to be his enforcer.

It had been hard work but now, twenty years later, it was all worth it. He was the big boss with twenty men and women working for him. He was involved with drugs, prostitution, and anything else that was shady and paid big money. Along the way, others had tried to usurp his place and take over his territory, but with the right incentives and a few bodies here and there, they soon backed off.

Now came along this twerp. Stack shook his head. If the kid weren't so stupid he'd almost have a future in this business. That is, if he ever managed to stay alive.

CHAPTER NINE

IT WAS LATE Thursday evening. Jessie stretched behind the wheel as much as the confined space would allow. It had been a long drive through four provinces. If her calculations were correct, she should be in Poplar Grove in half an hour. The long drive had been therapeutic for her. Still upset over everything that had happened with Linda, Jessie had finally been able to put it into some kind of perspective.

The problem with Linda had been going on for a very long time. Jessie had always known how Linda felt about her but she had never been so vociferous before. She had thought that with time Linda would get over it, that with maturity she would figure out how to put things into perspective. Obviously, she had been wrong.

The sign just ahead stated that Poplar Grove was another twenty kilometers away. Jessie moved her head from side to side, trying to relieve her stiff neck muscles. Somewhat comfortable again, she glanced at the speedometer. Only ten over the limit – not bad, that was about average for her. She continued her visual checks by looking in the rearview mirror and that's when she saw the flashing lights of the patrol car.

Oh great, just what she needed, some uptight Mountie trying to fill his quota of tickets for the day. Or maybe the cop was on his way somewhere else? With that hope in her head, she slowed and then pulled over to the side of the road.

Constable Jack Enders was not a happy man. Everything that could go wrong had gone wrong right from the start of his shift. When he arrived at the detachment he had found that Cliff had been released from custody. He had wanted to do that himself so he could have a friendly chat with the teenager. This was the second time Cliff had been picked up and Jack wanted to "scare him straight." He was annoyed and ended up arguing with the staff sergeant.

Enders left the detachment to begin his day; it was his month on highway patrol. He was ten kilometers from town when he got a flat tire. Halfway through putting the spare on, it started to rain. He hurried to finish and was just climbing back in the car when the rain stopped. Perfect timing or what?

Soaked and grumpy, he decided to make a quick stop at home to change into a dry uniform. As he pulled into the driveway, he was surprised to see his girlfriend's car parked there. She should have been at work but he shrugged it off, figuring something must have come up.

As soon as Enders opened the back door he knew something was up. He stopped just inside the door and cocked his head to one side and listened. At first he was disbelieving, and then he was angry. A few seconds later he was in the bedroom and there she was, bare-assed naked, riding some guy like he was a bucking bronco at the Calgary Stampede.

Without thinking, Enders grabbed him by the hair and dragged him off the bed while she just sat back where she had landed and stared at him, mouth hanging open. Enders dragged the man out of the house without a stitch of clothing and when he opened his mouth to ask for his pants, Enders just growled and held up his closed fist. The man got the message and ran.

When he got back to the bedroom, he told her to pack her stuff and get the hell out. He took a clean uniform from the closet and went in the bathroom to change. When he left she was still sitting on the bed, speechless.

For the next few hours Enders stopped a few speeders and wrote them tickets. Just about everyone he stopped gave him attitude or a sob story of one kind or another. His tolerance level was extremely low.

It was just about the end of his shift and he was on his way back to town. All he wanted was to get back to the detachment so he could write up his report and leave. He had been following the rusted out Ford with Ontario plates for a few kilometers and the driver hadn't slowed down. He turned on the light bar and followed the car as it moved onto the shoulder.

Stopped on the side of the road, Jessie dug out her driver's license. She reached over to get her insurance papers from the glove box. Just as she was straightening, she heard a tap on her window. Startled, she turned to see a RCMP officer with a billy club in his hand. She rolled down the window.

"Excuse me, miss," he said. "Did you know the posted speed limit in the area is ninety kilometers per hour?"

"Yes, sir, I do." He made Jessie nervous. The officer was tall and imposing, and with the hat and sunglasses, it was hard to see his face. She felt more intimidated than she ever had around the OPP.

"Would you care to tell me why you willfully disobeyed to speed limit?" His voice was deep and slow.

"Well, sir, just before I saw your lights I had glanced at the speedometer and noticed I was ten over the limit."

"And you didn't slow down? We have speed limits posted for a reason, young lady. I'll have your driver's license and registration." He thrust his hand out.

Jessie handed over the papers. She watched in the rearview mirror as he walked back to the cruiser. She tapped her fingers on the steering wheel, waiting. What could be taking so long?

He finally came back.

"I'll have to ask you to step out of the vehicle, miss," he ordered.

"What for? I haven't done anything." She couldn't believe this.

"Standard procedure."

Not only was Jessie very tired from all the driving but she was getting angry. Who did this big-jock cop think he was? She was only ten over the limit, what was the big deal? She threw open the door and recoiled in surprise when it swung back and hit her shin; now she was really mad.

"Standard procedure? My dad was a guard and in all his stories he never talked about this being standard procedure. What's going on here? It's not like this is a stolen car or anything, it's mine!" She slammed the car door shut.

Enders stared at her. "Are you quite done now?" he asked.

"Yeah, I guess."

"Now, I'm going to give you a ticket for speeding. The fine is seventy-five dollars. You can pay at the detachment in Poplar Grove. I'm going to follow you to make sure you do." He gave her back her papers.

"I can't believe you're giving me a ticket for only ten clicks over the limit. Not get your quota today, Mountie?"

"Listen, miss, you were speeding, I caught you; you get a ticket. That's the way it is." Now he was mad. "If you're going to argue about it, I'll haul your ass to jail and let you cool off."

"No one goes to jail for speeding. Who do you think I am, some no-brain bimbo?" She was beyond reason now. "Give me the damn ticket."

He handed it to her.

She grabbed it, held it up and slowly, deliberately, ripped it in half, then in half again.

"That's what I think of your stupid ticket," she said as she watched the pieces float to the ground.

"If that's the way you want it." He whipped out his handcuffs and slapped them around her wrists.

"Hey!" she protested. "I didn't say I wouldn't pay! What the hell are you doing?"

"What does it look like? I'm arresting you for abusing a police officer and for littering. It's against the law to litter; at least it is here in British Columbia." He put his face just a few centimeters from hers. "Now you can cool down in a cell. How do you like them apples?" he said, a cold, tight smile on his face. He grabbed her arm and started pulling her toward the police car.

"I can't believe this! What about all my stuff?" She tried to pull her arm from his grip. When that didn't work, she dug in her heels. "Someone will come along and steal my car. Hey!" She yanked her arm again. "I asked you a question! I at least need my purse."

Enders opened the back door of the cruiser and pushed her on the seat then slammed the door. He walked to Jessie's car and found her purse, closed the window and locked the doors.

"Your car will be towed to the impound lot for the duration of your stay," he told her. "I've got your purse here for you." He held it up. "Now, I suggest you shut your mouth and enjoy the rest of the drive to Poplar Grove." He started the car and pulled onto the road.

As soon as he had slammed the door behind her, Jessie's temper had given way to embarrassment.

"Look, Officer, I'm really sorry I acted like such a bitch. I've had a miserable week and I took it out on you. I'm sorry. Can we just forget this? Please?"

He ignored her.

Jessie couldn't believe that her first view of Poplar Grove was going to be from the back of a police cruiser.

As they entered town, she looked around. It seemed to be fairly large and looked nice, not that she'd get to explore it anytime soon.

The car stopped in front of the police station. She was herded in like a criminal. All through the booking process, Jessie kept apologizing to the officer but to no avail. She may as well have been talking to the wall. Before she knew it, a cell door was slamming shut behind her.

She couldn't believe it: in jail over a speeding ticket! She paced the cell for a short time then sat down on the thin mattress of the bunk. With her head in her hands, she went over the whole thing again. How stupid could she be, to pick a fight with a cop? The humiliation wasn't over though. Half an hour later, Enders came back and opened the door to her cell. With an evil grin, he told her she had to be searched.

"Searched? What for? Oh right, standard procedure." She shook her head and followed him out of the cell.

Fifteen minutes later she was escorted back to her cell. Jessie was mortified, her face still burning with embarrassment. At least they hadn't done a strip search. It had been bad enough though, having some woman feel her body all over. No secrets left there. But it was over now, thank God.

At eight o'clock the matron brought her something to eat. She wasn't very hungry, but ate anyway. She was told she'd be there overnight so she might as well try and get some sleep.

Tomorrow was another day.

CHAPTER TEN

"HEY, SARGE, WE need to take the dogs out and do some practice. Buck and I are heading to the impound lot. Slim was s'posed to stash some stuff for us. D'ya know if he did or not?"

"Yeah, George, he did." Constable Williams waved them out the door. "Now get out of here, I've got work to do."

"Yeah, yeah, we're goin'."

George and Buck went out and got the dogs from the compound behind the police detachment. After the trouble last year, Prince George RCMP had supplied the Poplar Grove Detachment with drug dogs. Ongoing training was required to keep the dogs and their handlers in shape.

"I sure wish we could have done this earlier," Buck complained. "I had to cancel my date tonight and you know how much I like Stacey."

"You mean, she finally took pity on ya," George teased him. "She's prob'ly relieved you cancelled! Havin' a few drinks to celebrate!"

"Aw, get off George, you're just jealous!" Buck took a good-natured swipe at George. They nattered back and forth while they got the dogs out of the compound. Both dogs were on leashes as they entered the impound lot, but once inside with the gates closed, the dogs were let loose.

"Okay boys, do your stuff!" Buck encouraged them.

George and Buck followed the dogs, chatting back and forth.

Before too long one of the dogs caught a scent and was scratching at the door of a rusted out Ford Escort.

"Hey, what's this?" asked Buck. "Slim knows he's not supposed to stash stuff in any vehicle's just come in. Do ya think he looked at this heap and figured, why not?"

"He knows better," George replied. "Let's mark it and go on. He may have tried to trick us though, the bugger. Where's Jamie?"

"Jamie!" Buck yelled. "Where are you boy?"

The dog barked in response. They followed the sound to an abandoned car. The dog was in the back seat, scratching furiously at something under the front seat. When they retrieved the package, they found it had the proper police markings.

"Good boy, Jamie." George patted the dog and hooked up his leash again. He straightened and said, "Well, isn't this interesting, Bucky. Methinks the boys stumbled onto something here. I doubt if Slim hid two packages. Just to be sure, though, give him a call. I'll take the dogs back."

Buck went back inside.

George headed back to the Escort, where he retrieved Max and put both dogs back in the compound, then went back in the detachment.

"Guess what, George, you were right." Buck told him. "Slim only hid one package. Looks like we've stumbled onto something. We'd better call the staff sergeant." Buck was beaming. It wasn't very often drugs got delivered to the police impound lot – in fact, not at all for the fifteen years Buck had worked there.

"Hey, Jack!" he yelled.

"What do you want Buck?" Enders asked, not really paying attention.

"Didn't you just have a car towed in tonight? Ford Escort, lots of rust?"

"Yes I did. What of it?"

"Well, George and I were out working the dogs just now? You wouldn't believe what we found." Buck stood beside Enders, grinning, and just waited for him to look up.

"What? All I saw was a bunch of garbage."

"Max found some drugs!"

"What's so exciting about that? Isn't that what the dog is supposed to do? It's nice to see someone doing their job around here." Enders stood up from behind the desk. "I'm out of here."

"That's not what I mean. It looks like Max found drugs in the Escort."

Buck could have knocked him out and Enders wouldn't have been more surprised. "You've got to be kidding. I arrested that girl because she was pissing me off. I figured a night in the can would teach her a lesson. She sure didn't seem the type." He shook his head. "You just never know." He headed for the door.

"Buck," George said, "I just talked to the Staff Sergeant. He said to call in Jenkins to handle it. Call him, will ya? He can come over in the morning. Since she's already locked up there's no sense paying overtime if we don't need to. I'll go out and secure the vehicle."

CHAPTER ELEVEN

JESSIE SLOWLY CRACKED open her eyes. What were those strange noises? And why was her bed so uncomfortable? The two gray walls and two other walls made up of bars quickly brought it all back. She was in jail because of a speeding ticket. She looked at her wrist to check the time then remembered they had taken away her watch.

"Guard! Guard!" she yelled.

After what seemed like an hour someone finally came. "What do you want?"

"Ma'am, could you please tell me what time it is?" Jessie brushed her hair away from her face. She looked at the matron; this one was different from last night and she didn't look like she was all that happy to be there. Well, neither was Jessie.

"It's eight."

"When do I get out of here?"

"When the staff sergeant says you do." The matron turned and walked away.

Jessie looked around to see if anyone else was visible. The coast was clear. Without wasting time, Jessie went to the bathroom. She hated it, but what choice did she have? At least she was in the cell by herself. Jessie took her time washing her hands and face in the stainless steel sink. Since she didn't have a toothbrush or toothpaste she did what she could using her fingers to scrub her teeth; it would have to do for now. Finished with her abbreviated morning ritual, she sat back down on her bunk to wait for her release.

Two hours had gone by before the staff sergeant came and opened her cell door and motioned for her to come out. He was a large man, tall and in good physical condition.

"Follow me, miss," was all he said.

Jessie shrugged and followed, determined to keep her mouth shut so she could get out as fast as possible.

She was put into a room and the door was closed behind her. There was a large mirror in one wall, most likely one-way glass. In the middle of the room there was an old scarred table and two chairs that looked like they had seen better days.

Jessie sat down and tried to figure out what was going on. The stories her Dad had told her didn't include being shut in a room as part of the release from custody procedure. She looked around for a few minutes, then, thinking this was crazy, she decided to look for the staff sergeant.

She tried the doorknob but nothing happened.

What's going on here? She wiped her hands on her jeans and tried again. It still wouldn't turn. It must be locked! She stood there staring at it as though it would tell her what was happening. Just as she was reaching for the knob once more, the door swung open hitting her hand. She stumbled back, wincing at the sharp pain in her fingers.

"What are you doing?" Staff Sergeant Jones asked.

Jessie rubbed her hands together, working to ease the ache in her right hand. She looked warily at the staff sergeant.

"What's going on here?" she asked again. "I thought I was being released. Why am I in this room?"

Staff Sergeant Jones waited at the door until a female officer walked in, carrying a chair. He waved her toward a corner of the room where she placed the chair and sat down. He closed the door and walked to the table, setting down a tape recorder, a pad of paper and a file folder.

"I suggest you come and sit down. I have a few questions for you."

Jessie slowly approached the table. With a questioning look she sat down opposite the officer.

"What's going on?" she asked warily. "Why do you want to ask me questions? I already apologized to the other officer for my behavior. I've learned my lesson. Can't you just let me go now?"

Jones looked at her. He didn't need this. Life was just getting back to normal, finally. He stretched his legs under the table, his large feet sticking out the other side. He was in his fifties, starting to go a little gray at the temples, still in good shape despite all the desk duty a staff sergeant had.

"Well, miss" – he looked down at the file, which was now open – "Ms. Lane."

"Yes, that's my name. Jessie Lane." He was making her feel nervous, but she didn't know why. She'd paid her little debt, what else was there?

"Ms. Lane, like I said, I have a few questions." He turned on the recorder. "This is Staff Sergeant Jones. It is Friday, June 10, 2008, 10:00 a.m. I am in interview room one with Ms. Jessie Lane and Constable Roberta Walkins who is observing. Ms. Lane, I will be taping this interview. Do you have any objections?"

"No, sir," she replied slowly.

"State your full name for the record."

She complied.

Jones wasn't quite sure how he wanted to proceed with this. Maybe some background questions to start.

"It says here that you were born in Wayne's Junction in Ontario. Is that correct?"

"Yes, but . . ."

"It also says that you were adopted in 1993 by Bob and Jill Lane. Is that correct?"

"Yes, that's right, but I fail to see . . ."

"I ask the questions, you answer them. It also says that you grew up in Blane, also in Ontario, and you graduated from high school and you work at a service station. True?" He looked up at her.

There was a look of confusion on her face.

"Where did you get all this information from? Why would you need to know all of this anyway?" She could feel beads of sweat popping out on her forehead.

"It doesn't matter where the information came from, is it accurate?"

"Well, yes it is. But again, I don't understand what is going on here." She looked around the room again, waiting for someone to walk in and say, "Surprise, you're on *Candid Camera*!" But another look at the officer across from her convinced her that this was for real. What could all this be about?

"The constable who arrested you tells me you have quite an attitude problem. Care to explain yourself?" He was trying to get a feel for her honesty and integrity.

"Like I told him, it's been a bad week for me and he just hit me the wrong way." She shrugged, "I said and did some things I shouldn't have. It was the last straw but I later apologized for my actions. Is that what all this is about? My bad attitude last night?" Relief flooded into her body and she almost smiled.

Jones read through her file again, stalling. From what he could see she didn't seem like much of a criminal. All the information they had on her led him to believe that here was a person who'd had a rough start in life but had managed to land on her feet. He'd have to keep digging.

"No, Ms. Lane," he finally answered, "that is not what this is about."

"What else could it be? I've done nothing wrong." Her face changed to a light shade of red, still feeling embarrassed. "Nothing else that is."

"What do you mean nothing else?" His abruptness made her tense up. "What else is there? What aren't you telling me?" He drilled her with his eyes.

"No-nothing," she stammered. "Nothing else."

Jones leaned back in his chair. He'd thought he'd had her there for a second. Either she was a very good liar or she had no idea what was going on. However, evidence was evidence.

"Well, Ms. Lane," he hesitated, "may I call you Jessie?"

"Yeah, sure, I guess," she said warily. "Does this mean you're going to tell me what this is all about?"

"Yes," he said. "The reason you're here, in this room, answering questions is because we found something in your car last night."

"Oh?" Jessie felt relief, again. "Find some money hidden in one of the door panels?" she joked.

Jones looked at her closely. "You hide money in your doors?"

She blushed. "I was just joking." Stupid, stupid, stupid, she admonished herself silently. She took a deep breath and let it out slowly. "As far as I know, the only stuff in my car is what I packed in it on Tuesday. I bought the car last year for a few hundred dollars," she shrugged. "I thought maybe you found some money or something. It would explain all the questions about my background."

Jones leaned forward on the table. "I wish it were that simple. No, Ms. Lane, Jessie, we didn't find actual cash but we did find something worth a lot of money."

Jessie was bewildered. What on earth could he mean? "What are you talking about?"

"We found a bag of cocaine stashed in the right rear door panel of your car. How do you explain that?"

CHAPTER TWELVE

"COCAINE?" JESSIE REPEATED, astonished. Her face lost all color. She grabbed the edge of the table, her fingers white from the pressure. "Are you sure? My car?"

"Yes, it is cocaine." He pretended to read from the report Jenkins had given him. "Found in the right rear door panel of a 1993 Ford Escort, light blue, lots of rust. The license plate is registered in your name; it is your car."

"I can't believe it." Jessie shook her head. "How would cocaine get into my car? I just don't understand."

Jones wasn't sure whether he believed her or not. He might be in Poplar Grove, otherwise known as Hicktown, B.C., but he hadn't been there forever.

Grant Jones was once stationed in Burnaby, a large detachment. He'd seen and heard it all. He felt in his gut that things weren't adding up here but until he had something provable, Jessie Lane was all he had.

"Listen Jessie," it was time to try another angle. "Don't try that shocked, 'I'm innocent' crap with me. I don't buy it. Those drugs didn't get in there all on their own. Now, I suggest you get yourself a lawyer, and if you can't afford one, I'll call the public defender's office."

"I don't need a lawyer," Jessie protested, waving her hands. "I've done nothing wrong."

"What I don't get is why you would pick a fight with a cop, knowing what was in your car. Are you looking for attention? Is that it?" He leaned forward and eyeballed her. "Well, Jessie, you're getting lots of attention now."

She didn't know what to do. How could this have happened? She sat in the chair, rocking back and forth, her arms around her waist, shaking her head.

"Am I under arrest?" she finally asked, her voice barely above a whisper.

"Yes, you are." Staff Sergeant Jones proceeded to read her the charge and state her rights. "Do you understand the charge and your rights?"

"Yes," she answered in a monotone. "What happens now?"

"I will rebook you, take your fingerprints, and then you'll go back in your cell. We have a warrant to search your belongings. You'll stay in the cell until you can be taken before the judge, which won't be until Monday. You can make a call if you want."

"Not right now, thanks, maybe later." All the fight had gone out of her. "Let's get this over with, please." All she wanted now was to be somewhere she could think. Normally that was sitting in the sun, but for now the only place available to her was the jail cell.

Jones ushered her from the room and the female officer followed along behind them. Jessie moved slowly, her feet heavy as lead. All through the booking and fingerprinting, she didn't say anything. Her movements were jerky and awkward. Finally, they were done.

The slam of the cell door made her jump. It was just what she needed to snap her out of the shock she was in. She paced the cell, her arms wrapped around her waist, trying to figure out what had happened.

She went over everything that had occurred over the last month. Except for the last few days, nothing stood out. She thought about all of her friends; no one she knew was involved with drugs, not that she was aware of. Who could it be? Linda? No. Linda was vindictive and mean but even she wouldn't touch drugs. Brant? No, that didn't make any sense either. Besides, Brant loved her; he had been in trouble in the past and had come to her for help. He had finished with gambling, he had promised her and she believed him. No, she was positive it couldn't be Brant.

Nothing was making any sense; her thoughts were swirling and churning around and around. She was exhausted and emotionally drained. She sat down on her cot and rested her head in her hands. She would be there for three days so she had plenty of time to figure things out. Slowly, she stretched out on the cot and pulled the thin blanket over herself before she fell into an exhausted sleep.

A few short hours later she woke up, covered with sweat and shaking. All she knew was that she'd had a bad dream, the details were unclear but the feeling stayed. For a few minutes, she lay still and tried to remember the dream, but soon gave up. Instead, she got up and stretched and banished the last unsettled feeling away. She looked through the cell bars and, seeing no one, she quickly used the toilet and then splashed water on her face.

She felt a bit better, more rested and a little more energized. The cell she was in was four feet by six feet with two walls of bars and the other two walls of concrete. The toilet was stainless steel with a small sink as part of the tank and it was located where the bars met the wall on the far side so you could have a tiny bit of privacy.

The walls were scarred with initials and rude comments. She hadn't paid this much attention to where she was before and she was wishing she hadn't done it now. Not wanting to dwell on where she was or why she was there, she sat back on the cot and thought about her family.

After the Lanes had adopted her, she'd finally begun to trust again. Just thinking about everything that had happened to her as a child gave her a chill. She wrapped up tight in her blanket, not noticing the itch it left on her arms.

Linda had been her hero for the first few years, until Jessie began to notice how jealous Linda was of her. She hadn't understood it then but now, from where she was sitting, things began to make a bit more sense to her.

Jessie had few boyfriends in school. She was shy around them at first but if they gave her a chance to know them, she quite enjoyed spending time with them. A short laugh escaped her.

Her first boyfriend, Jimmy, was as shy and awkward as she was. The first few times they spoke they would both stand there and look at the floor. If they chanced to look at each other at the same time, both their faces would glow bright red.

Thinking about it now, Jessie wondered how he ever got up the nerve to talk to her in the first place. She smiled and took a deep breath, then let it out slowly.

After Jimmy came Stan. He was more outgoing and they had a lot of fun together until Stan thought it would be a good idea if they 'went all the way.' Jessie wasn't interested so that was the end of that.

Then came Michael. A wistful look came to her eyes. He was by far the nicest boy she had ever dated. They were together all through senior year. For graduation they gave each other their virginity. It was the most romantic night of Jessie's young life. That fall, Michael moved to Vancouver to attend the University of British Columbia. Their summer together was one Jessie would never forget. They had tried to have a long distance relationship but they were changing too much too fast so they parted. When he came home he always called her and they would meet and catch up. Last time though, Michael had announced his engagement. Jessie was happy for him.

Every man she met since then had been measured against him and they had all come up short for one reason or another. Maybe it was time to change things, to let the past go. It was what she really wanted for herself.

Linda had only had one boyfriend. He was very nice, good-looking and lots of fun to be around but for some reason Linda didn't believe he loved her. She kept accusing him of secretly liking Jessie better.

Jessie would never have known about it except that Peter came to see her not long after he and Linda broke up. He told her about Linda's jealousy and how it had destroyed their relationship. She tried to talk to Linda about it, but she flew into a rage, so Jessie had decided to leave it alone.

She finally realized that all the things that had happened between her and Linda had contributed to their last big fight. Linda would have to figure this out for herself; there was nothing Jessie could do except let her know that no matter what, she loved her.

Jessie yawned and stretched again, then lay back down on the cot in the hopes that she would be able to finally get some proper sleep.

CHAPTER THIRTEEN

HE BOLTED UPRIGHT, sweat poured off his face, and his eyes sprang wide open. The last threads of the dream left his mind and caused him to shiver with the departure. He blinked several times in an attempt to bring the room into focus. Slowly, the world seemed to come back to normal.

It had been weeks since he'd last had the dream. He had been getting used to being able to sleep. He hated the dream, if that's what it could be called. It brought everything back. It had been almost a full year since it had happened, since his life had been ripped apart.

On shaky legs, he got up and went to the bathroom. He stood in front of the mirror and stared into his eyes. The anguish was there, like it always was after the dream. Only it wasn't really a dream was it? It was real, everything he dreamed about had happened.

He turned the water on, and, using his hands, splashed water onto his face. Three, four, five handfuls and finally he was beginning to calm down again.

In the kitchen he put a pot of coffee on to brew. He sat down at the table and tried not to think of that night or the events leading up to it. The coffee was ready.

Once his cup was full he went to the living room and sat down on the couch and rested his head on the back. He sat in the dark and sipped his coffee and tried to stay in the present; it was a losing battle. Before long his thoughts went back again, he couldn't help himself.

He felt a small smile escape. They had moved to Poplar Grove seven years earlier. Beth had just found out she was pregnant. They wanted to leave the city and make a life for themselves in a small town. They chose Poplar Grove because of its size and location. Less than a two-hour drive north of Prince George, its beauty had astounded them. The town was supported mainly by the forest industry, as were most towns in rural British Columbia.

They bought a small motel on the edge of town. Life was perfect; Beth worked hard to make a home for them and the coming baby while he got the motel fixed up. When Carly was born, they fell in love with her instantly.

The first couple of years went by quickly. The business did well, especially during hunting season. Hunters from all over North America came to try their hand at hunting moose, elk and caribou. There was plenty of fishing in the area with the many rivers and Williston Lake luring them to go after the big catches.

The police had come to him just over a year ago. Apparently one of his lodgers was suspected of drug trafficking. They wanted his help so they could arrest the man and his connection in Poplar Grove. Being a good citizen, he had agreed to help. If he'd known how it would all turn out, he never would have done it.

At first he didn't have much to do: monitor the movements of the man, keep track of who came in and out of his room, keep tabs on when the man left and returned to his room. It was harmless work, or so it seemed at the time.

This went on for two weeks.

Finally Staff Sergeant Jones told him they were planning to take the man into custody. They wanted him to keep the rooms on either side empty in case there was trouble. That was easy since it wasn't very busy at the time.

The night of the arrest, everything went smoothly. The man was arrested and taken away. Life went back to normal.

Three days later it happened.

Beth and Carly had gone to Prince George for a girl's outing and to do some shopping. It was the last time he saw them alive.

On their way home, according to the police report, they failed to negotiate a sharp curve. The car went over a cliff, rolled to the bottom and exploded in flames. There were no survivors.

He remembered it as if it happened yesterday.

He had just finished the books for the day when the police showed up. One look at their faces and he knew something horrible had happened. When they told him about the accident, he went into deep shock. He remained that way until after their funerals.

Then he became angry.

He went out to the scene of the accident. He followed the approach Beth would have taken. It didn't make sense, why would she miss the curve? The amount of marks the tires had left showed something else. He went further up the road. The marks started about two kilometers before the corner. Something was wrong. He followed the marks. At first they were spaced several meters apart: one kilometer from the corner the marks were getting closer together, meaning the brakes had been applied hard and often.

Why? Beth had driven this highway many times. She would have known she was approaching the sharp turn. She was a cautious driver, especially with Carly in the car. There was no way she would have driven wildly enough to make all these marks.

Someone else had to have been there. Who? Why?

Then it had come to him; the man that had been arrested. It had to be him or one of his associates. Someone was retaliating. Why his family? Someone must have found out that he had helped the police. How could that have happened though? Jones had assured him that his part in this would be kept quiet. This was crazy.

He went to see Jones.

Jones listened to what he had to say, he even went with him to look over the accident scene. While Jones agreed with him on his hypothesis, he also said there were too many other possibilities and no way to tell for sure that Beth was the one to make all those tire marks.

He couldn't believe it. Later on he went back yet again and took pictures of the marks and the trail the car had made going over the cliff. As far as he was concerned, his wife and daughter had been murdered and the murderer was still out there.

The police hadn't been able to find the drug connection in Poplar Grove since the man they arrested wouldn't talk.

He finished his coffee and set the cup on the coffee table. With his head in his hands he closed his eyes and saw the wreckage once again. With a groan he got to his feet. Since he was up he may as well shower and start the day; there wouldn't be any more sleep for him.

CHAPTER FOURTEEN

JESSIE WOKE WITH a start. She shook her head to clear it and looked around to see what had woken her. Staff Sergeant Jones had opened her cell door.

"Come with me," was all he said.

Jessie followed him to the same room she had been in the previous day. This time, Jones came in with her. They sat at the table across from one another.

"What's happening now?" Jessie asked.

It had been a long day previously; she still couldn't figure out what had happened. All afternoon and evening she had paced and thought, thought and paced. Nothing had made any sense to her. Now here she was back in the interview room. What else had they found? What was she going to be charged with this time?

"Jessie, we did some more investigating yesterday. We took your fingerprints and the prints off the cocaine and compared them."

"They didn't match, did they?"

He nodded agreement; "They were not consistent with you being the person who handled the package at any time, including stuffing it inside the door panel of your car."

"Thank God!" Jessie heaved a sigh of relief. "I told you I didn't do it!"

"Yes, you did say that." He looked at her thoughtfully for a moment. "But this doesn't clear you at all. You could still be involved. It doesn't mean you had nothing to do with it." He stood and walked around to where she sat. With one hand on the table and the other on the back of her chair, he towered over her.

"Who is your accomplice?" he thundered, scaring her. "Who were the drugs for, Jessie? Why have you brought them here?"

She had cowered in her chair while he was yelling at her, tried to shrink as much as she could. When he stopped she turned slightly to get a better look at his face. He was so close to her, she had to lean back.

"What?" she squeaked.

Jones pushed himself away from her. He didn't enjoy scaring people, especially women, but he had to figure this one out.

"You heard me young lady," this time at normal volume.

"I heard you, I just don't believe you. I told you I have no idea how those drugs got in my car. If I knew I'd tell you." Jessie could feel her eyes stinging with unshed tears. She fought to hold them back. Would this nightmare never end?

Jones looked at her for what seemed like an hour but was really only a few minutes, and then he seemed to make a decision.

"I *might* believe you," he said.

When Jessie seemed about to respond, he waved at her to keep quiet.

"We still have a ways to go," he continued. "I talked to the judge and he agrees. We are going to release you on your own recognizance." He shook a finger at her. "You are not completely out of the woods yet, though. We will be keeping your car as evidence and you can't leave town. Do you have a place to stay?"

"No, I don't." Jessie couldn't believe it; she was going to be released? Someone must be looking out for her. "If you remember, I hadn't quite made it to town yet." She didn't want to say anything about Mae just in case she didn't live there any longer.

"Yes, well, okay. I think I know a place you'd like. It's not expensive, but it is nice. Come with me."

They left the room. Jones returned Jessie's belongings to her, and after she had signed for everything, he escorted her to the compound and watched while she removed her suitcases from the car. They seemed bulkier than before. She lifted questioning brows at Jones.

"Remember, we had a search warrant. That included your luggage. These guys are not known for neatness."

With her purse over her shoulder and a suitcase in each hand, Jessie followed Jones out of the compound where he pointed out one of the cruisers.

"That officer will take you to the motel I mentioned. Make sure you check in regularly, and if I find out anything I'll get in touch. Remember, do not leave town." He turned and walked away.

Jessie walked over to the car, intending to get in the front seat. As soon as she saw whom the driver was though, she changed her mind and, with a mild groan, opened the back door. Once her suitcases were piled in, she followed and closed the door behind her, saying, "Please, not a word."

CHAPTER FIFTEEN

JESSIE FELT THE car slowing down and opened her eyes to take a look around. It hadn't taken very long to arrive at her new destination. "The Dew Droppe Inn," the sign read. As soon as Enders brought the car to a halt, Jessie got out, dragging her two suitcases with her. Without exchanging a word, the officer pulled away.

The motel was at the edge of town; the town wasn't as large as it had seemed Thursday evening when she first arrived. Down the street she could see a few stores and a restaurant. Jessie stood where she was and closed her eyes; her face pointed toward the sky, letting the sun warm her, and forced her mind to clear. There would be enough time later to think about her situation.

After a few minutes she turned and looked at the motel again. It wasn't very big; there were ten units with a patio running along the front and the office was at one end. Someone had hung flower baskets along the edge of the roof. Jessie inhaled deeply, the air smelled and felt wonderful, especially after the jail cell. With a smile on her face, she decided everything would be all right. With a suitcase in each hand, she headed for the office.

Jessie left her luggage outside and opened the door, a bell tinkling above her, startling her. She looked up in time to see the small bell swinging back and forth. With a smile and a laugh, she walked to the counter and waited.

She was just about the ring the bell on the counter when a man came out of the small office behind the counter.

"Hi, can I help you?" he asked. "Hope I didn't make you wait too long. I just had to finish adding up some figures. If I'd left them, I'd've had to start all over again." He smiled at her.

"Oh, that's okay," Jessie replied. "I'd like a room please."

"How long are you planning to stay?"

"I'm not sure but at least a week, maybe two." Hopefully things would be sorted out long before then.

"Okay, that would be fine. The rate is two hundred a week or thirty-five dollars a day. Take your pick." He smiled again.

"I may as well do the weekly thing, at least for the first week. Would that be okay?" Jessie noticed the man had nice blue eyes and when he smiled, it filled his whole face.

"That would be fine. By the way, my name is Dave Sterling, I own this joint." He smiled and stuck his hand out. "Any problems you just let me know."

Jessie shook his hand then filled out the registration card.

"You don't have a car?" he asked.

"Uh, not at the moment," she answered, blushing.

"Oh?"

"Look, I'd rather not get into it right now if you don't mind."

"Sure, I'm sorry, sometimes my curiosity gets the better of me." He looked down at the card again. "Please accept my apologies, Ms. Lane." He raised his eyes to meet hers. "It is miss, isn't it?"

"Yes, it is," she answered, blushing again. "Thanks." She grabbed her key and left.

When Jessie opened the door to unit number nine, she felt like she had finally found a refuge after being in a two-day nightmare. The first thing she did was take a long, hot shower.

She stood under the shower and let the hot steamy water pelt her skin as she waited for some of the tension to ease away. She scrubbed as hard as she could to get the last two days of jail off her skin, and by the time she was finished, she felt like a new person.

While she was unpacking her suitcases, she went over everything that had happened over the last few days. Who was behind all of this? It seemed everything had started with the fight between her and Linda. Could Linda really have done this? Jessie still couldn't believe that but one can never be sure since she was learning anything is possible.

She stretched out on the bed and went over the possibilities. Maybe she should try and call Brant. Maybe he would know someone who could have done this to her. She knew she was grasping at straws but she had to think of all of the possibilities.

One look at the clock beside the bed told her it was lunchtime and reminded her that she was very hungry. She got up and finished dressing and headed for the restaurant she had seen earlier. It was great just to be able to get out and walk. She smiled to herself. Freedom! There's nothing like it.

One hour later, she was back in her room and felt full and slightly contented. Stretched out on the bed, she decided to relax for a few minutes before phoning

Brant. When she opened her eyes, it was late afternoon and the sun was shining on her. Its warmth had woken her and it felt great.

In the bathroom, she splashed water on her face and studied herself in the mirror. She realized she felt much better even though she hadn't meant to take a nap.

The phone was on a small table by the large window that the sun was streaming through. With a deep breath she walked over to it and looked down at it, then mentally prepared herself to speak to Linda as she picked up the receiver and dialed.

She held the phone tightly as she waited for Linda to pick up. It rang five, six and then seven times. She was just about to hang up when it was finally picked up.

"Hello," Linda answered, breathless.

"Hi Linda it's Jessie."

Silence echoed back.

"Linda? Are you there? Talk to me please." Jessie rolled her eyes then looked heavenward. "Come on."

Again, nothing but silence.

"Linda, is Brant around?"

"No, he isn't, no thanks to you," Linda finally responded.

"What do you mean 'no thanks to me'? I haven't talked to him for days, not since before I left." Jessie shook her head in disbelief. What had gotten into Linda?

"He disappeared Thursday. I haven't seen him."

Linda seemed determined to drag this out as long as possible.

"Listen Linda, I'm sorry if you're still mad at me. Maybe I should thank you. I would like nothing better than to patch things up with you at some point but right now I really need to find Brant."

"Patch things up? Who says I want to? Why do you need to find Brant? Hope to poison him against me?"

Jessie could hear the sneer in Linda's voice. She took a deep breath and let it out slowly. It wouldn't help if she got angry right now because Linda would clam up.

"Look Linda, I'll get into it with you another time. Please, if you know where Brant is just tell me, please. I would really appreciate it."

"That's just it, Jessie. I don't know where he is." All of a sudden her voice was quiet and the sneering attitude was gone.

"You're serious." Jessie frowned; she felt fear tap on her shoulder. "What can you tell me?"

"The day you left, when Brant came home from work, we got into a big fight."

Jessie heard Linda draw in a ragged breath. Something bad had happened; she just knew it. "There's more Linda, I can hear it in your voice."

"Yes, there's more. Brant told me that because you had left town he was a dead man. What did he mean Jessie?"

Now it was Linda's turn to hear silence.

"Jessie? Jessie, what's going on?"

"Oh . . . my . . . god!" Brant *was* involved. "Linda did he say anything else? Anything at all?" Please, please, she silently begged.

"No, I don't think so," Linda seemed to have put aside her hostility, at least for the moment. "Jessie what's going on? I'm really worried."

"Linda, think!" Jessie urged. "Think hard! Are you sure Brant didn't say anything else?" What the hell was going on? She tried to think but nothing made any sense. Brant . . . and drugs?

"Wel-l-l, he said something about needing to find you. He came in real late Wednesday night and left before I got up in the morning, and I haven't seen him since. I'm really worried Jessie. I tried calling some of his friends but no one's seen him or his car since Thursday morning." Now the anger came back into her voice. "Jessie, if something has happened to him, it's all your fault!"

"Linda, I have no idea what's going on but I'm going to try and find out. If Brant's in trouble and it sounds like he is, it was none of my doing. When you have some time to think about it, you'll realize that. I'll call if I hear anything."

Jessie hung up the phone and then stood where she was, gasping for breath, unable to believe what she had just learned.

It was Brant! It had to be. But why? Why would he do something like this to her? Unconsciously she began to move about the room, trying to work it out. Should she call Jones and tell him about this? No, she couldn't do that, not until she knew what Brant had gotten himself involved in. What was he doing? What could he have been thinking of? After everything she had done for him! She slowed her steps, took in a deep breath and let out a loud scream of frustration.

What on earth had happened? She thought about some of the messes she had seen Brant get involved in.

When they were younger, it had seemed as if he was always in trouble for one thing or another. Things like spending money that didn't belong to him and "borrowing" Linda's make-up so he could change the dog into a raccoon. Jessie had managed to smooth things over for him, sometimes taking the blame herself; she just couldn't help it. He was such a cute little boy, he knew how to get around her and he always made her smile.

There was something more going on, she could feel it. How would she be able to find out and would she be able to fix it? Should she fix it?

CHAPTER SIXTEEN

JESSIE WAS WALKING in her room again. How was she going to find out about Brant? She knew a couple of his friends; maybe she could call them? Everything was swirling through her mind at warp speed, and nothing made any sense. What she needed was to get her mind off this for a while. This would be a good time to try and find Aunt Mae.

With a course of action in mind, Jessie looked around for a phone book, since that seemed the most logical place to start her search. She checked the drawers in the dresser that she hadn't used for her clothes, the desk, and even the closet and the bathroom. All she found was the requisite motel bible. What was the point in having a phone without a phone book? Jessie wondered.

The owner should have a phone book; he may even know Mae. No, she decided, she would only ask for the book.

This time when she opened the door she was ready for the noise of the bell. She walked up to the counter and waited, this time looking around to see what there was to see.

"Hello, Ms. Lane." He smiled at her. "What can I do for you? Is everything okay?"

"Hi, Mr. Sterling, yes, everything is fine except I can't seem to find a phone book in my room."

"Please, call me Dave, and sorry about the phone book, but you wouldn't believe how many get taken from the rooms. I never realized small-town phone books were such hot ticket items, so now I don't put them in the rooms." He shrugged. "What's this world coming to?" He reached under the counter and brought one out.

"Thanks," Jessie responded, laughing, "I'll just look at it here. I wouldn't want to be responsible for increasing the crime rate in Poplar Grove!" As soon as the words were out of her mouth she realized what she had said and felt her face change color. To cover up she quickly ducked her head and opened the phone book.

"You don't seem the type to be committing crimes," Dave joked back.

Jessie ignored him, her concentration focused on the phone book. She couldn't find any Mae Bennett listed there. Frustrated, she slammed the book closed and slid it back toward Dave.

"What's the matter?" he asked, a small frown creasing his forehead.

"I came here to find someone but she must have moved. She's not listed here. Damn!" Jessie felt her eyes water. She quickly turned away so he wouldn't see.

"Lots of folks around here have unlisted numbers. Maybe the person you're looking for does too."

Jessie smiled, "I hadn't thought of that." Then her shoulders slumped. "But that still doesn't help me very much."

"Well, maybe I can help you. I've lived here for a few years and I know pretty much everyone around here. Who are you looking for?"

Did she dare to hope?

"I'm looking for Mae Bennett."

"Mae Bennett? Let me think." After a few seconds he grinned at her. "Of course I know Mae! Everyone knows Mae."

"Really?" Jessie smiled. "Oh, that's great! Where does she live? Do you know her phone number? Do you have a piece of paper so I can write it down?" Finally, something was going to work out.

"Wait just a minute," he laughed as he held up his hands. "I do know her phone number but she's not here right now."

Jessie felt all her excitement drain away; knowing her luck these days, Aunt Mae was probably gone until fall.

"Do you know where she is?"

"The last time I talked to her she was heading to the coast to take part in a protest of some kind." He turned and looked at a calendar on the wall behind him. "I think she's supposed to be back in a few days."

Jessie frowned. She knew she would still be here a few days from now but that didn't make things any easier. She looked back at Dave, frustrated.

"How about I get us each a cup of coffee?" he asked. "You look like you could use it."

"Thank you, that would be nice."

"Do you take anything?"

"No, black is fine."

Jessie watched him walk away. He was a handsome man with dirty blond hair, blue eyes, and a muscular body. If only her life wasn't so screwed up right now, she might like to get to know him better. He seemed like a nice man. Hopefully, he'd tell her about Aunt Mae.

He brought out two cups of steaming coffee.

"Let's go out on the patio," he said. "It's such a nice afternoon."

"That sounds lovely." Jessie walked out ahead of him and took a seat. He sat down beside her and handed her the coffee.

"Thanks," she said, taking a sip. "This is really hitting the spot."

"You're welcome."

They sat for a while, not talking, just enjoying the warm spring sun. Slowly, Jessie relaxed.

"Dave, can I ask you a question?"

"Sure, Jessie. What do you want to know?"

"I was hoping you could tell me a little about my aunt. Do you know her well?"

"Yes, I know her." He looked away. "She's a terrific lady. I don't understand though, if she's your aunt, don't you know her?"

Jessie looked away from his prying eyes.

"Yes, she's my aunt." She took a deep breath, letting it out slowly. She looked back at Dave. "I haven't seen her since I was a little girl, I vaguely remember her."

"Oh?" He looked at her, encouraging her to continue. Jessie ignored him.

"What does she look like? I seem to remember long hair, a headband and lots of beads."

"That sounds like her all right," he laughed. "She's a handsome woman, a free spirit. That's the best way I can think of to describe her. Just being around her makes you feel like everything's okay."

"She sounds just like what I need right now." Jessie averted her eyes, realizing she may have given too much away. He didn't notice, or if he did he gave no indication of it.

"Well, if you need someone to help you figure things out, Mae is the one to do it." He sat there lost in thought.

"What else can you tell me about her?"

He looked at his watch.

"Look, I need to get a few things done to finish up for the day. Why don't I take you out for dinner later and I'll tell you everything I know?

Jessie didn't know how to respond. She really didn't know this man and didn't she have other things she should do?

After considering for a moment she realized she needed to keep her mind occupied with something other than Brant and the mess she was in. Dave was offering to tell her what she wanted to know about Aunt Mae, not take her on a date.

"Okay," she agreed, "but on one condition."

"What's that?"

"If I'm going to pump you for information, you have to let me buy you dinner."

"There's really no need . . ."

"I insist; it's the least I can do."

"Well, if you insist, then okay. Who am I to turn down a pretty girl?"

Jessie blushed in response.

"I'll just go and finish up," he smiled at her. "It'll take me an hour or so. Why don't you go around the back and look at my garden? I find it a good place to think and relax. I'll come get you when I'm ready."

"Sure," she said, as she watched him walk away.

CHAPTER SEVENTEEN

DAVE AND JESSIE entered the restaurant, the same one where she had lunch earlier. They seated themselves in the back, next to a large picture window overlooking the flower garden.

The waitress brought them menus and took their drink orders. While they waited they looked out the window, the silence between them easy and natural. Jessie felt more relaxed than she had in days.

"I . . ."

"You . . ."

They spoke at the same time and laughed.

"You go first," Jessie said.

"I was just going to say that you seem relaxed compared to earlier. The gardens must have helped; I knew they would."

"Thank you, yes, they did." Jessie smiled at him. "That's what I was going to say. It was just what I needed. Was I really that obvious?" she frowned.

"Not really," he was quick to reassure her. "I'm glad you're feeling better. Are you ready to order? The specialty is rainbow trout."

"I should probably look at the menu. I came here today for lunch," she said as she opened the menu then closed it again. "If you say trout, then trout it is."

Dave motioned the waitress over. "Jody, we're ready to order."

"What'll it be, Dave? Trout?" she asked.

"Yes, please, for both of us. You know me too well!"

The waitress smiled and walked away. Dave poured wine for both of them and then lifted his glass in a toast.

"Here's to relaxing." They touched glasses and drank.

"Tell me about Poplar Grove, I've never been here before."

"Poplar Grove got its start in the late 1800s, as a town that is. I think there used to be a small band of Indians who lived here at some point, although there aren't any here now. Most of them died off from white man's disease and the rest moved on. The odd one has come back and now lives up in the hills.

"There was a sawmill here and that brought people in to work. We are also in a great hunting area and over the years our reputation has grown. Now during hunting season, we get a lot of hunters here."

"What kind of wild animals are there around here?" Jessie asked.

"We have quite a variety actually: caribou, moose, deer, elk, black bear, grizzly bear, mountain sheep, many species of birds and small animals. It's really quite spectacular. Our days are long in summer and short in the winter.

"The downtown area is pretty much the way it's always been. Some changes have been made to the outside of the buildings and some businesses have come and gone. Normal changes that seem to happen anywhere."

As he was speaking, Jessie had noticed how his eyes beamed with pride and affection.

"You really love it here, don't you?" she asked.

"Yes, I do," he responded.

Just then, their dinner arrived.

After they had both eaten some of their food they resumed their conversation, moving on to other things. Jessie studied Dave as he talked. He was very charming and interesting. Her body tingled when he looked into her eyes, and described a deer that had been in his garden, the look full of excitement and intensity. She fought to suppress her body's reaction. With everything that was happening, she did not need to complicate her life with romance.

"Wow!" she exclaimed, trying to change her train of thought. "That was great! I didn't realize I was so hungry. This was a very nice idea, Dave, thank you."

"You're welcome, Jessie. And thank you," he replied, smiling. "I haven't had such a lovely dinner companion in a long time. Now, though, I bet you'd like to get back to the subject of Mae."

"Actually," she replied, "I was enjoying hearing about Poplar Grove, but now that you bring it up, yes, I'd like to hear more about my aunt."

Dave motioned for Jody to come over and ordered two coffees. They waited while she cleared the dishes off their table.

"Your Aunt Mae, as I said before, is a free spirit. I don't know how she does it. She's had more than her share of tragedy in her life." He shrugged. "I guess all that equilibrium has helped her out a lot, but I don't know all the details." He fell silent for a moment then took a deep breath, shook his head slightly as though to clear it, and then smiled at Jessie.

"Sorry, I just kind of went away there for a sec. Anyway, Mae owns an acreage out of town a ways. She has a log house that's really nice. She plants a large garden every year and uses it to feed half the town, I'm sure. And her flower gardens! They are a sight to see. Even this early in the season, they're beautiful. Right now, she's taking part in some kind of protest. Knowing Mae, it involves children or the underprivileged. She's always involved in that type of thing; she can't stand to see children taken advantage of."

Jessie turned away to hide the tears that threatened to spill down her face before she reached up to brush them away.

"Have I said something wrong?" Dave asked.

"No, not really," she replied as she turned back. "It's just what you said about kids, it just struck a chord with me, that's all." She took a deep calming breath. "Please, continue."

"Well, that's about all I can tell you about her, really. The rest you'll need to experience for yourself. Meeting and getting to know Mae is an individual experience." He finished off his coffee. "Would you like a brandy or something?"

"I think a brandy would be perfect, thank you."

He ordered the drinks and they continued to talk and get to know one another. He told her about deciding to leave the city seven years before and how it was a move he'd never regretted for the most part.

She told him about wanting to explore her roots. When he asked her why, she wasn't sure she should tell him. Wasn't that just a little *too* personal? Something, though, told her she could trust him, that maybe it would do her some good to talk things out. This wasn't a feeling she was very familiar with especially after the last few days. She decided to follow her instinct and take a chance. She lowered her head a little and studied her hands for a minute before she spoke again.

"I was adopted Dave. My adoptive parents were killed in a car crash two years ago. It was real hard to come to terms with it; I loved them very much. They gave me – well, it doesn't matter now." She stole a quick look at him; the empathy in his gaze gave her the courage to continue. "My adoptive siblings and I got on well, or so I thought. Linda had always resented me, though I didn't really see it until now. Anyway, we had a big fight and I decided it was time for me to find out where I come from. I remembered Aunt Mae and here I am"

She looked up at him, waiting but for what she wasn't quite sure. Had she said too much? Would he disappoint her?

"It must have been very difficult for you," he finally said. "I know where I come from; I'm part of a large family. I don't know what would have happened to me if I didn't have them." He reached across the table and put his hand over hers "You see I know about losing someone you love. My wife and daughter were killed in an accident a year ago."

The moment he put his hand over hers, Jessie felt a jolt run up her arm. When he told her about his own tragedy, her body reacted with empathy, and tears gathered at the corner of her eyes.

"Oh, Dave, I'm so sorry." She didn't know what else to say.

"I didn't tell you because I want you to feel sorry for me. I wanted you to know that I know how you feel." He pulled his hand away and she felt alone again. "Okay enough of that. Let's talk about something else." He smiled. "Have you seen any good movies lately?"

Jessie laughed and leaned back in her chair. She looked around the restaurant and noticed it was filling up. The people of Poplar Grove must be late diners, she thought.

As she scanned, she noticed a woman glaring at her, which was odd since no one here knew her. The woman looked very chic, dressed in a shimmering light blue pantsuit with a white silk blouse that showed off a nice figure. She was quite beautiful in an artificial way with porcelain white skin and a slender body with shoulder length straight jet-black hair. Jessie looked away again and listened while Dave talked about his favorite movie.

A few minutes later the woman made her way toward their table. She walked straight up to Dave and ignored Jessie.

"Hello, stranger," she drawled.

Dave looked up at her. "Claire! Hello, how are you?"

"I'm doing fine, thank you, Dave. I haven't seen you out in a while." She looked pointedly at Jessie. "Now I see why."

Dave's face flushed as he made the introductions.

"Claire, this is Jessie Lane. Jessie this is Claire Hyde, my accountant."

Jessie stuck out her hand while Claire nodded acknowledgement.

"Jessie Lane. You're new here. I've never heard that name before."

Jessie started to reply but Dave beat her to it.

"Jessie is staying at the motel for a week or so. She's come to see Mae Bennett. I was just filling her in on our Good Samaritan."

"Yes, she is that. So you're not moving here?"

"No," Jessie replied. "Just visiting."

"Welcome to Poplar Grove," Claire smiled. "I hope you enjoy your visit." She turned to Dave. "When will I be seeing you in the office again, Dave?"

"I'll be in sometime next week . Claire, would you care to join us for a drink?"

"No, thank you. I'm meeting someone, a potential client." She turned back to Jessie. "It was nice to meet you; maybe I will see you around." She smiled but Jessie could see the coldness in her eyes. Claire turned and walked away.

"Well, Jessie, it's getting late and I have to be up early tomorrow. Do you mind if we call it a night?"

Jessie was still staring at Claire's retreating back. She dragged her attention back to Dave. "No, that would be fine. I could use an early night myself."

As they stood up, they both reached for their wallets at the same time.

"I said I was buying dinner so put your wallet away," Jessie said sternly.

Dave held his hands up in surrender. "Okay, okay, I won't argue. Thank you."

"You're welcome." Jessie walked up to the cashier and paid the bill.

They walked outside to the cool evening air; the smells of late spring sharp and pungent. At the motel Dave walked her to her door and told her to have a good night.

In her room, Jessie flung herself across the bed and thought about everything she had learned that evening. Aunt Mae sounded like just the person she needed to talk to; she could hardly wait to meet her. Dave was a nice man; attentive, charming, attractive and he made her feel weak in the knees. It had been a long time since that had happened.

What about that woman, Claire? She looked like she had wanted to claw Jessie's eyes out but changed her mind when she found out Jessie was only visiting for a short time. Oh well, Jessie shrugged, not her problem.

She was just about ready for bed when Brant popped back into her mind; not that she had forgotten about him but she had managed to push that problem aside for a few hours.

With her robe closed securely around her waist, she stood looking out at the night sky. Thoughts once again were swirling around her brain until she once more forced them to be quiet, emptying her mind of everything except the night sky.

As she was panning the sky, she noticed a faint green hue to part of it. Intrigued, she pulled on her sneakers and went out to the porch. More than half the sky was visible now and Jessie caught her breath.

The sky was alive! Swirling ribbons of light were dancing across it. She had never seen anything like it before.

"Wow!" she exclaimed to herself.

"It is beautiful, isn't it?"

Jessie jumped at the voice. She turned and saw Dave sitting in a chair looking up at the sky.

"What is it?" she asked, breathless.

"This is called aurora borealis, more commonly known as the Northern Lights."

"They are beautiful. I feel like I could reach out and touch them!" Jessie turned back to watch the sky.

She stood there for a long time, mouth slightly open, turning her head constantly, hoping not to miss any of it.

The ribbons of bright green vibrated across the sky. Every once in a while one ribbon would join another and they would dance together. Soon, though, they would part and carry on their separate journey.

When the lights had finally lost their vibrancy Jessie turned away, intending to say something to Dave but he had already left. She went back to her room, locked to the door behind her and crawled in to bed.

Within minutes, she was fast asleep.

CHAPTER EIGHTEEN

CLAIRE HYDE WATCHED closely as Jessie and Dave left the restaurant. They had seemed very chummy to her. The force of her anger caused her eyes to narrow until they were barely open. She was so intent on watching them walk away that she didn't notice her dinner date sit across from her.

"Hello, Claire."

"Hello, Claire," he repeated, this time a little louder, when she didn't answer.

"Jack Enders," she smiled coolly. "You're late."

"Yeah, sorry 'bout that. I got held up at work. What's so important that you had to see me right away?"

At that moment, Jody arrived at their table to take their orders. When she left, Claire answered him. "What's this I hear about drugs turning up?" She smiled when Enders looked surprised that she knew about it already.

"How did you know about that?" he asked, and then he looked at her with suspicion. "And why do you care anyway?"

"Oh well, I hear about a lot of things." She waved her hand around, dismissing his questions.

Enders's eyes narrowed as he studied her.

"What?" she asked. Someone at another table caught her attention, and she gave a quick wave. When she turned back to her companion, the look in her eyes was ice cold. "Quit worrying about how I know, okay? Is it true?"

It was his turn to look away for a second. With a quick nod he answered her, "Does this mean we're even now?"

"I'll think about it. Oh, don't look at me like that. What did you expect? You should be more careful who sees you when you're off duty."

Six months earlier, Claire had been driving out of town on her way to her cabin on a small lake thirty kilometers to the north. She had almost rammed into the back of his cruiser when she had rounded a corner. She stopped the car, intent on yelling at him, but when she approached the police car, she was shocked to see Enders and his girlfriend in the back seat, and they were not there just to enjoy the view!

Mortified at getting caught, Enders had hounded her until she swore she wouldn't say anything to the staff sergeant about it; maybe now she would be "paid" for her silence.

Claire watched him eat his dinner. He kept glancing at her, but she kept her thoughts and feelings to herself. She wasn't letting him off the hook just yet. She had an idea that he could still be of some use to her. Besides, an extra set of eyes in the detachment was a good business move.

When they were finished dinner she got up and walked out, leaving Enders to pay the tab. After all, every man should pay for the privilege of spending time with her and still consider it a gift.

CHAPTER NINETEEN

T HE LARGE BLACK car pulled into Poplar Grove after it had been on the road since Thursday.

Stack was getting edgy. They had followed her for three days. Luckily she hadn't covered her tracks at all, so her trail was easy to follow. Still, it had been a slow process. Every town they came to they had to stop and ask questions. Every now and then they got lucky and she had been seen at the first place they checked. Now here they were in another small town and the search would continue.

Brant sat in the back seat, slumped over with his head hanging down. Stack looked at him with disgust. When he got his drugs back he was going to teach Mr. Brant a lesson he would not soon forget.

"Hey, boss, I'm hungry. How 'bout we stop at this greasy spoon here?"

"Jesus, Dickie, you're always hungry," he complained. "Yeah, I guess so, why not? Pull over, Mike," he ordered the driver.

As soon as the car stopped they all piled out of the car, glad to get out and stretch their legs. Except for Brant, who took his time.

While they ate they decided on an action plan for this town. Dickie and the driver would start at one end of town. Stack and Brant would start in the middle of the town and work in the opposite direction. They would meet back at the café in two hours.

Stack pushed Brant out the door ahead of him. There were a few businesses on the main street. They went to each of them and inquired about Jessie.

Haven't seen her, they all said.

Stack was confident they were telling the truth; he was effective at asking questions. People just naturally wanted to answer him honestly the first time for some reason.

They went back the way they had come into town. There wasn't much besides the businesses and a few homes. A block or two down the street was a gas station. They'd had lots of luck at those. Stack walked in and questioned the attendant. There was no sign of her.

Stack stomped out of the station, clearly disgusted. He walked up to Brant and slapped him across the face.

Brant held his cheek and looked warily at Stack through the tears that came quick to his eyes. "What was that for?" he whined.

"Just because," Stack retorted. "I can't believe we're gonna be stuck in this two-bit Podunk town looking for your stupid sister. Is there something you're not telling me? Is she in on this with you? Is that it? You know where she is, don't you?" Stack glared at Brant. This was not the first time these questions were asked.

"No, I don't," Brant was quick to answer, again. "And she has no idea, I swear." He cowered away from Stack.

Stack grabbed Brant's arm and yanked him along the street behind him. "There's a motel over there that we'll check out. And don't be such a baby; be a man for once why don't ya? Jeez, you disgust me!"

They headed over to the motel.

"'The Dew Droppe Inn,' what a stupid name. Come on." Stack pulled Brant up the steps and they went into the office. The tinkle of the bell made Stack look up and frown. "Stupid hick town," was all he said.

Stack walked up to the counter while Brant hung back against one wall. There wasn't anyone behind the counter so Stack knocked on the countertop.

"I'll be with you in just a minute," a man called out to them.

"Hey, I don't got all day there, buddy," Stack called back.

Dave walked out of the office to the counter. "What can I do for you?" he asked.

"I'm looking for someone, her name is Jessie Lane, and she's five foot six, slim build with wavy long brown hair. Have you seen her?"

"And who are you?"

"I'm someone who's looking for her. What's it to you?" Stack turned on all his "charm." "If you've seen her I suggest you tell me."

"Or what?" Dave glared back at him.

"Look, buddy, I asked you a simple question. It's in your best interest to answer me." Stack leaned over the counter until his face was just inches away from Dave's. "You get my drift?"

"Are you threatening me?" Dave stared back at Stack. "I don't take kindly to threats. If you're not here to rent a room I suggest you leave."

They glared at each other for a minute and then, reluctantly, Stack backed down.

"Yeah, sure, we'll leave. For now." Stack had a feeling this guy knew more than he was letting on. They would meet up with the other two; Stack had the beginnings of a plan.

As soon as they were out on the street again, Stack said to Brant, "He knows something. We'll be keeping an eye on him."

Back at the café, Stack and Dickie discussed the situation.

"We didn't find her," Dickie reported. "No one's seen her. Maybe she's gone further west and that guy in Prince George lied to us."

"No, he didn't lie. She's here; I can feel it. That guy at the motel was cagey but he's seen her, I know he has. The way he was sayin' nothin' told me somethin'."

"Why don't I go over there an' tune him up a bit?" Dickie offered.

"No." Stack shook his head. "We don't want to spook him. He may warn her we're looking for her. We'll have to watch the motel, see if she shows up. I've got a feeling she will. Let's go."

They got into the car and drove back to the outskirts of town where they could watch the motel and be out of sight. The waiting had begun.

After a couple of hours of nothing happening, they began to feel edgy. Brant had been slowly looking around but not really paying attention. He noticed someone walking down the street toward the motel. He blinked his eyes to bring them into focus on the individual. It looked like it could be Jessie.

It was Jessie! He stole a quick glance at Stack beside him; he hadn't seen her yet. Stack hadn't met or seen Jessie before so recognition would be slower for him. Brant fought the urge to jump out of the car and run to her.

Stack had noticed Brant tense up. He wanted to know why so he looked around, first inside the car. When everything in there looked fine, he looked outside. He saw a woman walking toward the motel; he focused on her and saw that she fit the description. "Well, well, what did I say? It's about time, there she is boys!"

"That's her?" Dickie asked.

"It's gotta be," Stack answered. "She fits the description and Brant here is all tense. Bingo! Mike, once she's in her room, drive around the motel and we'll see if we can spot her car."

Five minutes later, they were idling down the road. They saw an old pick-up and two newer cars, but no rusted-out Escort.

"Damn!" Stack exclaimed. "Where the hell is the car?"

"Maybe it's at the garage for repairs or something," Dickie offered.

"No, it's not. We were there and I would have noticed it. Okay, we need to find somewhere to regroup." Stack tapped his fingers on his knees while he thought.

"Why don't we stay at the motel here? Keep our eye on the girl?" Dickie was proud of himself for suggesting it.

"We can't. We were in there earlier and the owner didn't much like our company. I can imagine what he'll say or do if we walk in and ask for a room. No, the least visible we are the better. We'll have to think of something else."

"Oh, hey," Dickie said after a few minutes of thinking. "I think I may know someone who lives here. This may be where John Domer lives now."

"John Domer?" Stack asked. "The same Domer who skipped town on me? He's here?"

"Oh, shit." Too late Dickie realized what he'd done. Oh well, Domer wasn't family or anything and they needed a place to stay.

"Yeah, that's the one."

Stack narrowed his eyes as he thought.

"Yeah," he finally said. "Why not? It looks like Poplar Grove is going to be the place where a lot of scores get settled."

The smile on his face would have scared his own shadow.

CHAPTER TWENTY

MIKE PULLED THE car to a stop in front of a rundown shack. The guy at the gas station had given them directions. The yard was full of garbage and old car parts. The four men got out of the car and slowly walked up the sidewalk. Stack shook his head in disgust. "JD certainly did not come up in the world," he commented.

They climbed the stairs to the front door. Each one of them skirted the missing piece of one of the steps. The screen door was open as it clung to the frame by its top hinge. Stack knocked on the door.

A young, pretty woman answered. "Hello," she said, "Can I help you?"

"Yeah, we're lookin' for JD. He here?" Without waiting for an answer, Stack pushed his way past the girl and the others followed him in.

"Hey, wait just a minute," she protested. "What do you think you're doin'?" But the girl was no match for Stack; she swung sideways with the door. One look at Stack's face told her not to argue. "He's in the back room." She waved them toward the back of the house.

Stack, with the others following him, headed in that direction. He followed the hallway and looked into rooms until he came to a closed door, which he threw open. There lay John Domer, passed out on his bed.

"Wake him up," Stack ordered.

Dickie shook Domer but got no response. Mike, the driver, went out to find the kitchen and came back with a bowl filled with cold water. Dickie threw it in Domer's face; that did the trick, and he woke up sputtering and spitting.

"What the fuck is goin' on?" he yelled as he fought to wake up and sit up. He wiped water out of his eyes then focused on the people standing around his bed. As he recognized Stack, Dickie, and Mike, his eyes got bigger and the fourth person he just dismissed. "Holy fuck! What the hell are *you* doin' here? Stack, uh, it's uh, good to see ya, man. How's it goin'?" He threw a worried look at Stack. They hadn't parted on the best of terms; he had taken off with some of Stack's money.

"Shut up, JD. Lucky for you we're here for another reason. I wouldn't waste my time looking for you. But since I've found you . . ."

The fist he hit Domer with surprised both of them. Stack, that he'd actually done it, since he usually left the beatings to someone else. Domer, that he'd actually let anyone do that to him. Domer's head whipped around with the force of the blow.

It felt so good that Stack hit him again, this time making Domer's head snap back the other way. Then he motioned for Dickie to finish him off.

When Dickie moved in, he pinned Domer to the mattress and hit him again and again. The only sounds in the room were Dickie's grunts and Domer's flesh giving way. Finally Stack called for a halt; Domer's debt was paid.

"Okay, asshole," he said, "now you're gonna help us with something."

Domer sat up, spitting blood and pieces of teeth. He grabbed the bed sheet and used it to staunch the flow of blood from his nose. He tilted his head back and through eyes already swelling, he looked at Stack.

"All right," he growled. "I had that coming to me." He spit out another piece of tooth. "Can I go to the can and clean myself up a bit now?"

"Yeah, all right, go ahead."

Domer stood up, keeping his head tilted back. He let go of the sheet so he could pinch his nostrils closed. He stood, weaving for a moment, and then made his way to the bathroom.

In the meantime, Brant was fighting the urge to throw up. He'd never seen anyone being beat up before. Every time Dickie hit Domer, Brant had felt it; well, almost. He took long deep breaths to settle his stomach.

"What's the matter with you, you little shit?" Stack spit out at Brant. "You never seen anyone get beat up before?" It was like Stack could read Brant's mind. "That's not near as bad as you're gonna get if we don't find that dope. It may happen anyway." Stack stalked out of the bedroom; they all followed along dutifully to the living room.

Domer's girlfriend had tucked herself into a corner of the couch, hands over her ears and tears streaming down her cheeks. When she saw Stack come in the room she asked him, wide-eyed, "Wha, what did you, uh, do to him?"

"Nothing he didn't deserve, sweetheart. He'll live. Go get us something to drink," Stack ordered.

She got up and stayed far across the room from them as she headed to the kitchen to do his bidding.

Everyone found a place to sit and wait.

Half an hour had passed by the time Domer made it to the living room, his face full of marks, both eyes swollen almost closed, his hair still wet from a shower. He was a big man, over six feet tall, and he filled out his shirt like a linebacker. Through the slits of his eyes he looked at Stack. "Okay, Stack, what do yuh want?" His words came out sounding like his mouth was full of rocks from all the broken teeth.

"We need some help to find some dope."

"Don't you have your own suppliers?"

"That's not what I mean, asshole." Stack got to his feet and paced. "This piss-ant," he gestured at Brant, "tried to rip some coke off me. He stashed it in his sister's car but then she split. We followed her here. We found her but not the car. Have you got any ideas?"

"Whoa," Domer said, his arms in the air, his hands up with the palms facing out. "He's still alive? Holy shit." He shook his head in disbelief. "You say you've seen the girl but not the car? How much dope was in it?"

"Never mind him," Stack glowered, "yes, we found her, staying at a motel here in town." Stack intentionally ignored the question of how much.

Domer tried to frown but his face was too swollen for anyone to notice the expression. He tapped his finger against his lower lip while he thought.

Finally, "What's the car look like?"

Stack had Brant describe it to him and the Domer left the room.

A few seconds later there was a loud scream and then they heard Domer yell at his girlfriend to shut up. Not long after that the girlfriend showed up with beer for everyone. After serving it she left the room. A few more minutes went by before Domer reappeared.

"I talked to a buddy of mine with a tow truck. He'll check around and get back to me."

Stack turned away from the window where he had been standing and staring. "We'll wait till he calls," he announced.

It was an hour before the phone rang; Domer went to answer it. When he came back into the room he relayed that he had good news and bad news.

"Just spit it out," Stack demanded.

"Well the good news is that he found the car. The bad news is that it's in the police impound lot."

"Damn! What the hell's it doing in there? We need to find out if the cops found the stuff." He looked at Domer again.

"I'll see what I can find out. Denny didn't mention anything. How much was there and where was it stashed?"

Again, Stash motioned to Brant to answer. "Tell him," he ordered, but hoping Brant would only say where it was stashed, not how much it was.

Brant told Domer where he'd hidden it. Like a dog with a bone, Domer asked again how much and Brant told him.

"One kilo?" he repeated, the expression on his face incredulous. "You came all this way for one kilo of coke? Are you nuts?" He turned to Stack.

"Just never mind why," Stack retorted. "Find it, that's all you need to do."

Domer left the room again and when he came back he told them he probably wouldn't hear anything until the next day. Then he offered to put them up for the next few days.

CHAPTER TWENTY-ONE

JESSIE HAD SPENT the day exploring Poplar Grove. She had tried again to call some of Brant's friends but she'd had no luck, and so she decided to go for a walk.

Poplar Grove was an old town. The houses dated back to the late 1800's. Most residences were off the main street, except for a few between the motel and the commercial district two blocks up the street. There was a garage one block up on the opposite side of the street from the Dew Droppe Inn.

The business part of Main Street was made up of an assortment of stores. The hardware store, grocery store, a beauty parlor, the restaurant she and Dave were at the night before. There was also a drugstore, a bookstore, two places that sold odds and ends, and a pub at the far end.

The further she got from the center of town, the more run-down it became. Some of the houses looked rather creepy, so Jessie decided to end her exploring of that part of town and she headed back toward the motel.

Twenty minutes later, she was almost back. Sunday was very quiet with no traffic to speak of. She noticed a car parked along the edge of the road past the motel. It was probably someone trying to figure out where they were. *Pretty hard to get lost in a town this small!* she smiled to herself. She continued on to the motel.

Back in her room, she tried calling some of Brant's friends once more. This time she was a bit more successful, but they all said the same thing: they hadn't seen or heard from Brant since Tuesday, but they had heard that someone was looking for him.

Jessie slumped down on the sofa, not sure what to do next.

She awoke with a start. The phone was ringing. Groggily, she staggered over to answer it.

"Hello?" she croaked out.

"Jessie? Is that you?" a voice whispered.

"Hello? Who is this?" she demanded.

"Jessie, it's me, Brant."

"Brant? Is that really you?" What on earth was going on? She hadn't told anyone back home where she was.

"Yes, Jessie. I don't have long to talk, if they found out I'd called you, they'd kill me."

"Who would kill you? Brant?" He was scaring her. "What's going on?" His voice was barely a whisper and she realized she was almost shouting. She lowered her voice. "Do you have any idea the trouble I'm in?" Her heart was racing.

"Yeah, sorry about that. Jessie, I need to see you. I'm going to have to try to sneak away, can you meet me?"

"Meet you?" Jessie rubbed her eye. "Do you know where I am? Of course you do, or else you couldn't have called me," she answered herself. "Where are you?"

"I'm in," he struggled. "I'm in the same place you are, wherever that is, somewhere in B.C."

"You're in Poplar Grove?" She couldn't believe it. "How in the world did you get here?"

"Yeah, that's the name. It doesn't matter right now how I got here. I don't have a lot of time. I'm in some guy's house, it's real run-down, but I don't know the specific address."

"I think I know the area you mean, I was out that way earlier, although I didn't venture too far in to the neighborhood."

"Look, I can't explain anything right now but I will, I promise. Just meet me somewhere. Assuming I can get away, that is."

Jessie tried to think of a meeting place in a hurry but nothing really came to mind.

"Why don't I head in your direction," she finally said. "You take a walk and head toward the main street. I'll find you. I'll leave right now."

They agreed on her plan and Jessie hung up. She looked at her watch; it was six o'clock. With her jacket in her hand she headed out the door.

Twenty minutes later, she was back in the seedy part of town. With no real idea of where Brant was, she started to walk up and down the street, moving over one each time.

"Jessie!"

She turned to see Brant running toward her.

"I don't have much time," he said, out of breath when he caught up to her. "I told them I needed to get some fresh air. If I'm not back in fifteen minutes they'll come looking for me." He grabbed her in a bear hug.

Jessie hugged him back then held him at arm's length, studying him.

"Brant, what's happened? You look terrible." At first she was concerned, and then she was angry. "What the hell is the matter with you? Drugs? How could you do that to me? Jesus, Brant, I could still be sitting in jail right now. I may end up having to go back. This had better be good." She stood back with her hands on her hips and looked at him expectantly.

"What can I say?" he asked before he hung his head low. "I screwed up again." He used his foot to move a pebble around in a circle, then he looked up at Jessie.

"I don't have a lot of time," he continued. "Okay, I messed up, and now I've mixed you up in it as well. I had no idea you were going to split town. Everything would've worked out just fine. I put the package in your door panel, just for the night! I had a buyer all lined up and everything. But now they're after you. They want their stuff back. Where is it, Jessie?"

She stood there and stared at him. At that moment, she didn't know who he was; he had made it sound like this was all her fault!

"I can't believe you, Brant," she wanted to scream at him, but fought to keep her voice under control. "You did this, all of this, on your own. Now you're trying to make it sound like it's my fault!

"The cops have your dope, Brant." She held up her hands to stop his questions. "I got stopped for speeding and I mouthed off to the cop so he arrested me and threw me in jail. That night they were doing some kind of training with dogs when they found your stuff in my car. My car! How could you?" She slapped him then, surprising both of them, and then wiped moisture from both her eyes.

"You just don't understand, Jessie. Look, I deserved that, but I can't stay and sort this out with you right now, I have to get back. Just keep a low profile, okay? You say the cops found it? I'm dead for sure." With that he turned and moved down the street.

Jessie stared after him. What had really happened? She still didn't know; all she did know was that Brant had gotten her in this mess. He didn't say one word about how he was going to get her out of it.

She turned around and headed back to the motel.

CHAPTER TWENTY-TWO

JESSIE SAT ON the steps outside her room to enjoy the spring evening. She leaned her head against the post that made up part of the patio railing, closed her eyes and took in a deep breath. What had she just learned?

Brant was in Poplar Grove. How he had gotten there, she had no idea. He had made it clear he wasn't alone; whomever he was with didn't trust him, that much was clear. He needed to get the cocaine back, but that was impossible now.

What could she do to help him?

Should she help him?

If she was really honest with herself, hadn't she contributed to this situation? If she hadn't bailed him out every time he was in trouble, maybe he would have learned his lesson by now. Would it be in her best interest to just forget about him? How could she do that and still live with herself?

She couldn't.

If only there were someone she could talk to, but there wasn't. The only thing she could do was go with her gut, which meant help him out of this mess and thereby help herself. First, though, she had to figure out if there *was* any way to help him. She went over what she knew from the beginning.

Somehow Brant got his hands on a kilo of cocaine and then he hid it in the door panel of her car. By the time he was ready to move it, she had left town. Now he was in Poplar Grove trying to get the drugs back. A person or persons unknown brought him here, presumably because the drugs belonged to them.

The problem, though, was that the drugs were in police custody. There was no way to get the bag back short of stealing it, which she immediately dismissed as ludicrous. Without the drugs, was there any way to help Brant?

He was going to have to turn himself in, which was the only way. If he did that, he would be protected and she would be exonerated. It was the only solution that made any sense to her.

Now, she would have to convince Brant. She just couldn't bail him out this time. She would do all she could to help him get through this but that was all. She would have to find out where Brant was and convince him to turn himself in, or else wait until he contacted her again and talk to him then.

She felt better having come to a decision.

Jessie smiled to herself with satisfaction and reopened her eyes just in time to see Dave walk across the parking lot. She felt that spark again just at the sight of him. Her hand lifted in an automatic greeting but Dave seemed to ignore her and continue on his way.

She frowned in response, unsure what to make of the snub. Just the day before they were getting along fine; getting to know one another. What could have happened to change that, she wondered. Her first instinct was to just shrug it off but something was drawing her to him.

Without conscious thought, she jumped up and followed him. As he rounded the corner of the building Jessie caught up with him.

"Dave?" Jessie grabbed his arm and stopped him.

He pulled away from her and scowled.

"Dave, are you okay? What's wrong?" She looked closely at him as he continued to scowl at her.

"I don't know," he finally said. "You tell me."

"Tell you what? Tell you what's bothering you?" She laughed and it sounded hollow, even to her. "How would I know? What's going on?"

"I'd really like to know. You told me you were here to find your long-lost aunt. Now someone tells me that's probably a crock. Just what kind of game are you playing?" He grabbed her arm and shook her.

It was Jessie's turn to pull away.

"How dare you? Don't touch me!" She rubbed her arm, trying to figure out what he knew. "I am here to find my aunt. Just what kind of game do you think I'm playing?" she threw his words back at him.

"I wish I knew." He ran his fingers through his hair.

"Dave, what's going on? Last night we were getting along real well."

"Yeah, well, I got a call from Claire this afternoon. You remember Claire? You met her last night."

"Sure, I remember, she looked daggers at me till she realized I was only visiting. What about her?" Jessie looked up at him.

"She had some interesting information to pass along. Any guess what it was?"

Of course she knew what it was but she play dumb. "Now how would I know? I don't know Claire. Why don't you just tell me?"

Dave glared down at her. "She was talking to one of the cops last night. It turns out there was some excitement here a few days ago. Yeah, some broad mouthed off Jack Enders, something about a speeding ticket. Jack, of course, arrested her and threw her in jail. And guess what they end up finding in her car? Cocaine. Cocaine! Does any of this ring any bells, Jessie?" He grabbed her again. "Does it?"

When she didn't answer right away he continued his diatribe.

"And then some jerk comes here looking for you."

Jessie snapped her head around at that bit of news. "What?"

"Yeah, some little twerp who thinks he's some kind of hood showed up with a scared young man. He wanted to know if you were staying here. I told him nothing," he was quick to add when she raised her brows in question.

"So that's how," she said softly. She had looked away but now turned back to Dave. "In answer to your question, yes, Dave, this does 'ring some bells' as you so eloquently put it." Her face had turned red; at first with embarrassment, then with anger. She drew herself up tall then wrenched her arm from his grip.

"You have no idea what really happened. What business is it of yours anyway? Who are you, the town know-it-all? Decider of who's good and who's bad? Well?"

Dave stepped back in surprise; he hadn't expected the attack. "Why didn't you tell me any of these things? I think I have a right to know."

"What right?" she demanded. "Just because I'm staying here at your motel? That doesn't give you the right to know my personal business!"

"I have a right to know what goes on in my own place," he shot back.

"No, you don't," Jessie retorted as she turned and walked away.

CHAPTER TWENTY-THREE

HOW DARE HE make judgments about her? He had no idea what was going on, and besides, it was none of his business! She headed for her room and then changed her mind. It wasn't very often that she turned to alcohol in times of stress, but tonight was different. She headed for the pub at the other end of town.

As soon as she walked in the door she stopped. She couldn't see a thing so she waited while her eyes adjusted to the gloom. As the room slowly became visible she took it in. Ahead and to the left were small round tables with chairs; to the right was the bar itself, taking up most of the wall. Past the bar were the doors to the washrooms. Jessie decided to sit at the bar, so she made her way there and took a stool. She wiped her face with her hands, working at slowing her heart rate, still racing from anger.

As she waited for the bartender, she smoothed back her hair and looked around. The pub wasn't very full; only a few people sat at tables and two people were playing pool. Finally, the bartender ambled over and asked for her order.

"I'll take a double vodka, straight up."

He whistled through what was left of his teeth and shook his head slightly, poured the drink and handed it to her. She grabbed the glass and tossed the drink back in one swallow.

"Wow, lady. Bad day?"

Jessie frowned at him. "Give me another, on the rocks this time. And I'll take a Bud as well."

"Comin' right up."

Jessie watched as he poured her drink then walked to the cooler for her beer. He looked like he was in his fifties; what hair he had was turning gray. He was bowlegged and walked with a slight limp.

"Here you go, miss."

"Thanks." She laid a twenty-dollar bill on the bar. "Keep the change."

This time, she sipped the drink, and when she was done, she reached for the beer and turned to survey the clientele once more. She watched the two men playing pool for a few minutes until she became aware that someone was staring at her. In an attempt to be casual, she turned slowly around and spotted a man sitting by himself at a table along the far wall. He was looking right at her, but she didn't know him; she kept turning.

"Hi there, come here often?"

The man had walked up behind her and sat down on a stool beside her. Jessie turned to look at him. He was tall and maybe good-looking, in a jock sort of way. The swelling and bruising on his face made it hard to see his features. He had black wavy hair worn shoulder length.

"No, I don't," she answered him. "I came for a quiet drink, and I'd appreciate it if you'd leave me alone." She turned away again.

"Aw, come on," he persisted. "We don't get many newcomers here. How about I buy you a drink? You look like you could use one."

Jessie looked at him again. He seemed nice enough, and she really didn't want to be alone with her thoughts.

"It looks like I should buy you one," she gestured at his face.

"Yeah, well, it looks worse than it feels," he lied. "What about that drink?"

"All right," she relented, "just one."

"First, let me introduce myself, my name's John Domer, my friends call me JD," he took her hand and shook it. "I'm pleased to meet you."

"My name is Jessie Lane, pleased to meet you."

Domer's eyes widened at the name but he quickly recovered.

"Come on over to my table, it's a little more private." He ushered her over and sat her down. He signaled the bartender for another round. After the drinks were served he lifted his in a silent toast.

"You're new in town aren't you?" he asked. "I would have remembered someone as pretty as you."

"You're quite the charmer, aren't you?" she responded, blushing. "Especially since you already made note of the fact that I'm not from around here." She laughed at him.

"You caught me." He lifted his hands in mock surrender.

They chatted amiably for half an hour. Domer tried to find out why Jessie was in Poplar Grove but she managed to dodge his questions. She felt quite comfortable with him in a meaningless sort of way. When he suggested they go out for dinner, she agreed. Anything was better than being on her own right now.

After dinner they went for a walk. Domer told her about the various shop owners, making her laugh at some of his observations. She had told him where she was staying and soon they were standing before the door to her room. Jessie thanked him for a lovely evening and said goodnight.

CHAPTER TWENTY-FOUR

DOMER HEADED BACK to the pub for another drink. Stack would be happy; he'd gone to the pub to drown his sorrows and had ended up finding the girl. Half a block away from the pub he heard someone call his name.

"Who's that lookin' for me?" He turned around and, seeing no one, turned back again. "What?" he jumped, slightly.

Brant had stepped out of the shadows when Domer had his back turned.

"What the hell are you tryin' to do? Give me a heart attack or somethin'?"

"What were you doing with her?"

"With who?"

Brant gestured toward the motel. "Her."

"What's it to you?" Domer moved to go past Brant, who reached out to stop him. Domer stopped, more from surprise than Brant's strength. He looked at Brant with narrowed eyes. "You better have a good reason for doing that, pal. I've a mind to bop you one but you look like someone's already beat the shit out of you a couple of times." Domer pulled his arm from Brant's grasp.

"Look, I just want to know what you were doing with that girl."

"It's none of your business," he said, ready to make good on his threat to hit Brant, but then he decided to play along. "Look, if it'll make you happy, I met her at the pub. We had dinner and took a walk. Now, tell me what was so important you had to know that."

"Jessie is my sister," Brant managed to squeeze out through clenched teeth. "Stay away from her, okay? Just keep your scummy hands off!"

Domer's eyes widened as much as the swelling would allow. "*The* Jessie?" he exclaimed. "The one Stack is looking for?" As if he didn't know that already.

"Yes," Brant admitted. "She has no idea what's going on, so just leave her alone."

"Or what punk?" He pushed past Brant. "Why don't you just screw off?" he said as he walked away.

He managed four steps away before Brant flew at him. The force and surprise knocked them both into the alley. Domer felt Brant on top of him, swinging his fists. One, two, three he felt on his upper chest. They didn't hurt because Domer was well-muscled. Brant let another one fly, this time catching him on the left cheek.

Domer let out a roar, pushing Brant off him.

They both got to their feet.

"Okay, punk. You asked for it." With the last word barely out, he went after Brant. The first punch was to his stomach, which knocked the wind out of him. Next he got Brant with a right upper cut to the jaw and a left to the side of his face. Brant fell to the ground on his back and struggled for breath. Domer turned and bent over in an attempt to bring his own breathing under control. He felt the left side of his face; it would look even uglier by tomorrow.

He was so busy feeling around for more loose teeth he failed to hear Brant come up behind him. The crack of the two-by-four on the back of his head was the last sound he heard before his body hit the ground.

Brant felt for a pulse, afraid he had killed him. When he finally found one he stumbled farther into the alley and vomited. When the dry heaves were finally over, he stumbled out of the alley.

Domer had no idea how long he had been there by the time he came to. He had a vague idea of nighttime and a deep throbbing pain in the back of his head. As soon as the ground stopped moving he tried to get up. He managed one slow bit at a time, fighting the dizziness with each step.

He was almost ready to try to stand when he became aware of a new danger; his body wouldn't or couldn't obey his commands to stand up. He shook his head to clear it then groaned with the pain. He felt something at his back and lifted his head a fraction in an effort to move away.

That movement was just enough to get the rope around his throat. Domer tried frantically to claw it away, any pain he felt all of a sudden forgotten now that his life was at stake, but his coordination wasn't there. He felt something up against his back and then the pressure hard against his neck. Slowly the blackness overcame him until he was no longer aware.

CHAPTER TWENTY-FIVE

BRANT KNEW HE had to get away and get to Jessie.

He got lucky; Stack left to meet up with someone and took Mike with him. Dickie stayed behind with him and Domer. Soon, though, Domer took off to do some business of his own, leaving Brant with Dickie and the girl. Dickie had a thing for Domer's girlfriend, so as soon as Domer left, he began talking to her. Susie ate it all up, you could tell, 'cause she was all shy and awkward around him. Dickie decided he wanted some privacy, so he told Brant to hit the road. But not before giving him a warning: "Be back in two hours or I'll break your arm."

Brant took off for the motel without a second thought. He had to talk to Jessie; she was the only one who could help him. Maybe she would be able to get enough money together to pay off Stack. In any case, he had to see her, if only to feel safe for a while. She was his haven.

He knocked on the door to her room but she didn't answer. Frustrated, he waited for a while and then gave up. He was across the street from the restaurant, on his way back to the house, when he saw Jessie come out with Domer. His first instinct was to run over there and yank her away from him but he needed Jessie on his side. After all that had happened, who knew what kind of reaction he would get if he interfered with her?

He followed her instead.

She walked around for a while with Domer and when they headed for the motel he didn't know what to think. He heaved a huge sigh of relief when Jessie said good night to Domer at her door.

Brant hurried down the street and hid in an alley to watch for Domer. When Domer came close enough Brant crept out of the shadows and confronted him; they ended up in an argument.

Brant started the fight; he swung wildly at Domer more than once and eventually hit him in the face. His head was thrown back and he roared at Brant, shook his head slightly then charged him. Brant took a punch to the stomach, which knocked the wind out of him, and then Domer finished him off by hitting him in the face. Brant felt the blood trickle out of his nose. He lay on the ground and tried to catch his breath. Domer turned away and bent over. As Brant shakily pulled himself upright, he felt a piece of wood with his hand. He closed his fingers around it and with the last bit of strength he could muster he hit Domer on the back of the head. Domer collapsed on the ground, unconscious.

Brant took a few deep breaths through his mouth; his nose was plugged with thickened blood. He felt his face with trembling fingers; he couldn't believe it! His poor face! He'd be lucky if he kept his looks, assuming he survived at all. He pulled himself the rest of the way upright and looked down at Domer.

In the little shaft of light coming in from the street, he could see blood coming out of Domer's head wound. With a quick spasm he bent over and threw up, the heaves so great his back arched. Finally, after what felt like an hour, he was done. He wiped his mouth with the back of his hand and stood up, weaving slightly. With a quick glance at Domer, he lurched out to the street and made his way to Jessie.

CHAPTER TWENTY-SIX

IT TOOK HIM half an hour to get there. He had to stop to catch his breath every few steps and he had to make sure no one was following him. He pulled himself up the steps to Jessie's room. After a few minutes and lots of deep breathing, he knocked on the door. When she opened the door all he did was stumble through the doorway.

"Oh my god, Brant!" Jessie looked out the door and, seeing no one, quickly closed it. She took his arm and guided him to the couch. "What happened to you?"

"I was in a fight with Domer." He looked up at her with hurt in his eyes. "What were you doing with him?"

"How do you know John? How do you know we were together? Were you spying on me?"

"No, I wasn't spying on you." He winced as he shook his head. "I managed to get away to see you. I came here and you were gone. I was heading back to his place, which is where I'm staying, when I saw the two of you together. How could you, Jessie?"

Jessie slowly sat beside him.

"How could I what?" she finally asked him. "I was in the bar and this guy started chatting me up. He seemed harmless enough and I didn't feel like being alone. We went to dinner and then went for a walk. So what?"

"Jessie, he's bad news. He's involved with Stack and Dickie." He put his head in his hands and moaned. "Have you got any aspirin? My head is killing me."

"Come on," Jessie said, helping him off the couch. "I'll clean you up in the bathroom, and then give you some aspirin."

Back on the couch, they talked for a while about their situation. Jessie made it plain to him that he should turn himself in to the cops but he wasn't having any of that. After he cooled off, they talked of other matters. Soon, though, Brant realized he'd have to get back and asked her to call a cab for him. He was going to be late but he hoped Dickie would take it easy on him.

The taxi pulled up in front of Domer's house, Brant got out, paid the driver and then made his way in the house.

Dickie started yelling at him as soon as he got in the door until he got a good look at his face; his left eye was swollen shut and both sides of his face were covered with abrasions. Dickie shook his head and let him go. Stack wasn't back yet, so everything was okay.

CHAPTER TWENTY-SEVEN

Monday morning, Jessie woke slowly and stretched her tired muscles. She felt as though she hadn't slept at all. As she lay there the previous evening came back to her in a rush. It had been just what she needed, to be with someone just for a few laughs. That is, until Brant had shown up at her door, beat up and angry.

As soon as she'd opened the door he'd let her have it.

She had ushered him into the room and closed the door. As soon as she had him in some proper light she saw the dried blood under his nose and the little bits of vomit on his chin. "Let's get you cleaned up and then you can tell me what's going on."

She pulled him into the bathroom and sat him down on the edge of the bathtub while she cleaned his face up. Every wipe of the cloth caused him to wince.

Once they were back in the main room, Jessie didn't wait before demanding some answers. "Okay Brant, what's up? What happened to you?"

"That guy you were with tonight? He's bad news Jessie. Stay away from him! He's with Stack and Dickie."

"How do you know who I was with tonight? Were you spying on me? And who are Stack and Dickie?" Jessie got to her feet and paced the room. "I can't believe you! You're the one in trouble here and you're watching me? Get real!"

"Jessie, you don't understand," Brant pleaded with her. "Please, just trust me! John Domer isn't anyone you really want to know."

Jessie eyed Brant with suspicion. "Is that what happened?" she waved her hand toward his face.

"Yeah, I had a few words with him. I think he got the picture. He won't be bothering you anymore."

"Brant, he wasn't 'bothering' me in the first place. We had a couple drinks and dinner and then we walked around town. No big deal." She took a deep breath. It was now or never. "Brant, you're going to have to turn yourself in."

His eyes wide with panic he sprung off the couch. "Are you kidding? I can't go to jail!"

"What's the alternative?" she argued. "There's no way you're going to get those drugs back, you must know that. At least in jail you'll be somewhat protected." She walked over to him and put her arms around him. "Brant, I love you. I wish you would tell me how this all started." The look he threw her made her back off. "Okay, okay, you don't have to tell me, not yet that is. Don't you see the only way is to come clean to the cops?"

Brant pushed himself away from her. "You say you love me. Why do you want me to go to jail? Not a chance in hell!"

Just thinking about it now made Jessie feel angry and defeated. She'd said her piece, now it was up to Brant.

While she got ready for the day ahead she tried to decide what to do. There wasn't anything she could do about Brant right now. What about trying to find Aunt Mae? Dave had told her she should be back this week; maybe she would be back early. It was worth a try. She picked up the phone and dialed.

"Hello," a soft voice answered.

Jessie was so surprised to get an answer she didn't know what to say at first.

"Hello? Is anyone there?"

"Uh, hello," she finally said. "Is this Mae Bennett?"

"Yes it is. Who is this?"

"Uh, I don't know if you remember me but my name is Jessie, Jessie Lane. You may know me . . ."

"Jessie! Little Jessie. Of course I remember you," Mae interrupted. "Oh my!"

"I, uh, I wondered if maybe we could meet?" Jessie's voice was little girl small.

"Of course. Where are you dear?"

"I'm staying at the Dew Droppe Inn."

"You're in Poplar Grove? I'll be right there."

"Actually, can we meet at the restaurant in town?" For some reason unknown to Jessie she wanted their first meeting to be somewhere else.

"Yes that would be fine," Mae replied. "I can hardly wait. Let's say in one hour? Oh, Jessie, you can't know how long I've waited for this!"

"An hour sounds good, see you then."

They had hung up before Jessie realized she might not recognize her aunt. From what Dave had told her Aunt Mae probably hadn't changed all that much from what she remembered.

Jessie inspected herself in the mirror. She was both excited and nervous. In the mirror she saw a young woman with long, wavy brown hair that was a little on the frizzy side. She grabbed for her hair spray and knocked over her perfume and make up in the process. Would her aunt be disappointed? She smoothed her hair and checked her clothes. Did she look okay? She had on jeans and a light-blue cotton blouse. She hurried back to the main room and tidied up just in case they came back to the motel.

Jessie looked at her watch; there was still half an hour until their meeting. It would only take five minutes to walk over to the restaurant. She sat on the couch to wait and got up a minute later. She remade the bed then went back to the bathroom to make sure everything was either put away or neat and tidy.

She couldn't take the waiting any more. With her jacket in her hand, she went out the door. A quick glance at her watch showed she still had fifteen minutes to go. She would take her time getting there, maybe window shop on the way.

Jessie was two doors away from her destination when she saw a beat up old VW van pull into a parking spot. Her heart began beating double-time. She watched as an older woman got out of the vehicle. The woman looked to be in her sixties; her long graying black hair was pulled back in a ponytail and she wore a long cotton dress with a flower pattern. Over the dress she wore a leather vest with tassels across the front of the shoulders and across the back. On her feet were hiking boots. It had to be Aunt Mae! All the old feelings flooded back. This woman loved her, she was sure of it. Without another thought, Jessie went running to her, her arms wide open.

"Aunt Mae!" she cried and she crushed her with a big hug, her tears coursed down her cheeks.

"Oooff! Jessie? Oh, Jessie." Mae returned the hug and then pushed herself away. "Let me look at you. My, what a beautiful girl you've turned out to be." Mae smoothed back Jessie's hair; then, using her thumbs, wiped the tears from her cheeks and hugged her again.

When they were finally seated in the restaurant, Mae asked Jessie to bring her up-to-date on her life. Jessie told her everything, except what had happened when she got to Poplar Grove.

"My life has been good, Aunt Mae. It got off to a rocky start but I'm doing okay. Something happened last week to make me realize that I needed to find you, to help me learn about myself, so here I am."

Mae reached across the table and put her hand on Jessie's arm. "I know it can't have been easy for you," she said. "You've been on my mind all these years. I knew you had been adopted. Jill kept me up-to-date on how you were doing; she was such a lovely person."

Jessie felt her eyes well up again. "Yes, she was. I miss her terribly. I miss them both."

"Well, that's it then, Jessie. You're coming to stay with me," Mae stated.

"I don't know if I can do that. There are a few things I haven't told you. I'd rather not say anything right now but I'll have to check with someone first. Why don't we go back to the motel? I'll make my call there."

"Sure. Whatever it is, you tell me in your own good time, if you want to, that is."

They walked back to the motel and Jessie suggested Mae wait for her in the garden while she made her call.

"Staff Sergeant," she said when she had Jones on the phone. "It's Jessie Lane. Are there any new developments?"

"Look, Jessie, I can't talk right now, I've got my hands full. There's nothing new yet. Is that all you wanted?"

"Actually, no. I wondered if it would be okay for me to stay with my aunt. Her name is Mae Bennett."

"I know Mae, but I'm sorry, I'll have to insist you stay where you are. Mae is too far out of town, and I want you nearby so I can keep an eye on you at least for the time being. Now, if that's all, I really have to be going."

"Yes, thanks, that's it." She hung up the phone, disappointed but not particularly surprised.

Jessie found Mae weeding the garden.

"I don't know how David thinks these flowers are going to grow if they're choked out by weeds. I thought I'd keep myself busy while I waited for you. Well?" Mae picked herself up and rubbed the dirt off her hands.

"I'm sorry, Aunt Mae, but I'm going to have to stay here for now. Hopefully that will change in a few days and I can come stay with you then."

"Oh, that's too bad, Jessie. Well, all in good time."

They walked around the garden for a while, admiring the flowers until they came across a bench, where they sat. For a while they didn't talk, just enjoyed each other's company. They were sitting there, holding hands, when Dave came along.

"Hello, ladies," he said.

"Why, hello, David, it's nice to see you." Mae stood and gave him a kiss on the cheek.

"Mae, it's nice to see you again. How was your trip? Who did you save this time?" he smiled at her.

"It was wonderful. We managed to raise quite a bit of money for the Child Find organization. You know my niece, Jessie?" she asked.

"Yes," he answered. "Hello, Jessie, how are you?" he asked her, on the verge of sounding rude.

"Hi, Dave. I'm great, now that my aunt is here." She looked at him pointedly.

"Yes, well." He turned as if to leave, and then changed his mind. "By the way, I just heard some disturbing news. There was a murder last night."

Both women gasped.

"Oh my," Mae said. "In our town? What happened? Was it anyone we know?"

"I don't know if you know him or not, Mae. His name was John Domer." When he heard Jessie gasp he looked at her. "Did you know him?"

"I, I met him last night," she stammered. "We had a couple drinks together then went out to dinner. He seemed like a nice enough person." Jessie's face was drained of color.

"Really?" Dave raised his left eyebrow in question. "Well, anyway, apparently he was seen fighting with someone last night. His body was discovered early this morning by someone walking their dog."

CHAPTER TWENTY-EIGHT

JESSIE HAD BEEN standing while Dave relayed the news. At his last statement, she sat down hard on the bench and put her hand to her mouth. "Oh my god," she gasped.

Dave frowned at her.

Mae watched the two of them and saw the spark that raced between them even if they didn't acknowledge it.

"Are you okay?" he asked.

"Oh, yes, I'm okay," she answered. In an effort not to give anything away, she forced herself to recover her senses quickly. "I just can't believe that someone I just met is now dead." She visibly shivered.

"O-kay." Dave didn't sound like he believed her. "I need to get back to work. I'll talk to you ladies later." With one last long look at Jessie, he turned and walked away.

"Bye, David," Mae called after him. "Be sure you get someone to weed these flower beds for you."

"Yes, ma'am," he answered and waved as he was going.

Mae turned her eyes to Jessie and looked her over carefully and thoughtfully for a few moments. "Are you okay, Jessie?" she finally asked.

"Yes, yes, I'll be okay." Jessie fought to bring her attention back to Mae, but she was thinking about Brant; wondering if he could have murdered Domer.

"You know, Jessie, David lost his wife and daughter a year ago."

"Yes, I know. He told me."

"Really? I'm surprised. That is very interesting, since it's not something he usually talks about. Let's walk some more," she suggested.

"Sure, okay." They made their way through more of the gardens. "What do you mean he doesn't talk about it?" Jessie finally asked, intrigued. She was busy looking at the ground and so missed the knowing gleam in her aunt's eyes.

"David thinks there's some mystery to it. Did he tell you any of the details?"

"No, not really. I had told him about Mom and Dad and he was just letting me know that he knew what it was like to lose someone you love." Jessie looked at her aunt. "Was there more to it?"

"Do you like him?" Mae asked instead of answering her question.

Jessie blushed in reply. "Yeah, I guess, except when he's making assumptions he shouldn't be making."

"I noticed a little spark between the two of you back there."

"Oh, that. Well, we had an argument, a difference of opinion; the assumption thing. I do like him though," she admitted. "But I don't see how it can go anywhere."

"I think you're just what he needs." She held up her hands to stop Jessie from saying anything. "I know we haven't seen each other since you were a little girl, but I feel I know you quite well from Jill.

"I'll tell you what I know about the accident; it may or may not help you. There's a lot I don't know, but I spent a fair amount of time with David after it happened. He seems to think it wasn't an accident. He thinks that whoever caused the accident did it to get back at him. For what, I don't know. He thinks someone drove them off that road. I'm not sure if he's just grasping at straws in an effort to explain away what happened. I do know he believes it. You'll have to ask him about it."

Jessie was quiet and thoughtful for a while as she mulled over this new information.

"What can you tell me about him," she finally said, "aside from the tragedy?"

"He's a very nice man. He was devoted to Beth and Carly. He works hard at his business and contributes to the community. He's always willing to lend a hand to someone in need."

"You make him sound rather boring, Aunt Mae." She smiled at Mae.

"Oh, boring he's not," Mae laughed. "My own observations? I think some girl would be lucky to have him love her." She put her hand on Jessie's arm, stopping her. "Are you that girl, Jessie?"

"I don't know, Aunt Mae. I need to get my life in order before I think about something like that."

"Love isn't always convenient, my dear."

They resumed their walk about the garden.

"What about you, Aunt Mae? Here we've been talking all about me and you really haven't told me about yourself. All I really know is you're my father's sister. I vaguely remember you coming to visit when I was little. Dave told me you're involved with underprivileged children. Tell me about your life, please."

"All right, Jessie. I guess I never really thought about it. Where shall I start?"

"Tell me about when you were my age."

They had made their way to a large tree in the back yard. The afternoon sun was warm; the air was full of insects hurrying about their business. Jessie and Mae chose a patch of shade and sat down on the grass.

"Actually, I'll start a little before that. When I graduated from high school, I decided that I wanted to go to university. My parents couldn't afford to send me, so I worked for a full year before I applied. I decided I didn't want to stay in Ontario, so I applied at the University of British Columbia and Simon Fraser University. I was accepted at Simon Fraser and I was offered a scholarship." Mae looked wistful for a moment, as she was lost in the memory.

"I wanted to be a teacher," she continued. "I loved kids and thought teaching would be very fulfilling. I enjoyed the university experience and that's also where I met my husband, Art. We married just after I graduated.

"Art was just starting his law practice. I took a job in an elementary school in Burnaby. We were so happy. Both of us wanted the fulfillment of children of our own but it wasn't meant to be. I miscarried three times before I was forced to give up the idea of children. It was heartbreaking."

Jessie reached out to touch her arm, and then held her hand. Mae's eyes misted over.

"I made my students my children," she nodded as she spoke. "It wasn't the same but it was fulfilling. We had just celebrated our tenth anniversary when I got the call." She looked at Jessie, tears gathering in the corners of her eyes. "Art had been in an accident; he didn't survive. I was devastated. It took me a long time to come to terms with his death. Finally, though, I did." She turned and smiled at Jessie. "That's when I came out to visit. Mom and Dad were both really sick and I wanted to spend some time with them and I wanted to meet you. You were such a pretty little girl. You followed me everywhere I went. I could see that Jim and Maureen weren't looking after you. I offered to take you, but they refused. Not refused, they demanded money for you." She looked at Jessie to gauge her reaction but Jessie just shrugged.

"Not that I wouldn't have done it," Mae was quick to add, "but before I could figure out how I would do it, Jim came after me with a two-by-four."

Jessie gasped in shock.

"He beat me pretty badly Jessie. When I had recovered I came to get you, but they had moved and I couldn't find you. I had no idea what happened to you until I received a letter from Jill telling me what had eventually happened. I knew you would be safe and I thought another change might hurt you more than help, so I made sure to keep in touch with Jill. Then Jill and Bob were killed. I wanted to contact you, but I felt that maybe I'd let too much time pass and you wouldn't want to see me, that I'd bring back all the bad memories." She squeezed Jessie's hand.

"I didn't know, Aunt Mae. Mom never told me that she kept in contact with you. Maybe she was waiting to tell me; I don't know." Jessie dried her eyes then put her arms around Mae and hugged her close.

They sat that way for a while and then Mae pulled away so she could continue her story.

"I took early retirement from teaching. I decided that I was going to spend the rest of my days fighting for the rights of children and to help ease their pains. When I'm not doing that, I have my garden. My life has been full and now I have you again." She smiled at Jessie and they hugged.

Jessie felt comfortable with her aunt, as though she'd known her all her life. It would be so easy to unburden herself to Mae, but was that really a fair thing to do? She decided it wasn't.

"Aunt Mae, I would like to tell you what's been going on here but I can't, not just yet. When this is all over though, I would like to spend some time with you if that would be all right."

"Jessie, of course. I'm not going to pry, so you tell me about it in your own good time. Just remember, if you need me, you know where to find me, no matter what." Mae got to her feet. "Now I have to go. My cow, Bessie, has been sick, and I need to check up on her. I don't like to leave her alone for too long."

They walked together to Jessie's room to say good-bye.

"Let me know when you can come and stay, Jessie. You're always welcome; I'd love to spend lots of time with you."

"Thanks, Aunt Mae, you can't know how much this means to me."

"I have a fairly good idea, dear."

Out on the patio in front of her room, they hugged each other good-bye. Jessie watched as Mae walked across the parking lot and up the street to her van.

CHAPTER TWENTY-NINE

DETERMINED TO GET some answers, Jessie headed for Dave's office. The ring of the bell was just an annoyance when she opened the door this time. As she stood at the counter she called out to him.

"Oh, hi, Jessie." He looked less than happy to see her.

"Oh, don't hi me," she snapped. "What do you know about what happened last night?"

"What do you mean? All I know is what I told you." He had stepped back, surprised by her anger.

"I don't believe you," she shot back at him. "The look in your eyes was enough to turn me to stone. What gives?"

"Oh, all right," he said, angry as well now. "I saw you last night, walking around with that goon. I saw him bring you back to the motel. You know Jessie, I never figured you for a one-night stand."

Jessie gasped as if he had slapped her.

"How dare you?" she snarled, her face red. "You have no idea what type of person I am. I enjoyed an evening with someone I had just met, just like I thought you and I had. Were you watching me? Keeping track of my every move, spying on me? Well?" If she'd had time to wonder she would have questioned why what he thought was so important to her. As it was, though, all she knew was that she was hurt by his obviously low opinion of her.

"No, I wasn't spying on you," he replied. "I just happened to see you, that's all."

"What else did you see? Anything interesting?" The steam had gone out of her anger all of a sudden, because now she wondered if he had something to do with the murder.

"No, I saw nothing else. Look Jessie," he had calmed down as well. "I don't know what's going on. I hear you're involved with drugs and now someone is dead, someone who is known to deal drugs. It doesn't make sense; you just don't strike me as someone who would be involved in this shit." He studied her face for a moment. "What's going on?"

Jessie's breathing was almost under control. She walked over to the window and stared outside, unseeing, trying to sort out her warring emotions. Dave didn't seem the type to commit murder, she was sure of it; but what did she know about murderers? Her gut told her he was okay and since she had absolutely no idea what to do now, maybe he could help her. There were too many angles that she couldn't wrap her head around on her own.

"Okay, Dave, you're right, this isn't like me." As she turned back to face him she realized that once she decided to trust him, she couldn't turn back. "I need some help but I don't know where to turn."

"Jessie, whatever I can do, I'd like to help you."

"Can I ask you something first? It's something Aunt Mae said to me." Her eyes darted away. "She told me that you think your wife and daughter were murdered. Is that true?" She stole a quick look at him.

"What?" he said, the surprise evident in his tone.

"You heard me. Do you think your wife and daughter were murdered?"

"I can't believe she would tell you that!" Just like that he was angry again. "That's not something I want to discuss."

Jessie could tell he struggled for control so she decided to drop it, at least for the time being. "Okay, I won't push. I hope, though, that you'll tell me about it sometime."

"Yeah," he replied, "maybe I will." The relief was audible.

"Can we go somewhere we won't be disturbed?" she asked. "I really don't want anyone to overhear this."

"Sure, come with me." Dave led the way through the office to his living room where they sat on the sofa, one on each end.

"Okay, Jessie, tell me what's going on."

"I'm not sure where to start." Jessie rubbed her hands on her jeans. "As I told you the other night, I was adopted and two years ago my parents were killed." When she looked over at him he nodded to her, encouraging her to continue.

"Last week I got in a big fight with my sister, Linda. Some nasty things were said by both of us. Suffice it to say, I decided I would have to leave so I came here to find Aunt Mae so I could figure some things out." She got up and paced around the living room.

"I wasn't far from here when I was pulled over for speeding. I was tired and bitchy and I mouthed off to the cop." She waved her hands in the air. "I know, not the smartest thing to do. Anyway, he hauled me to jail to let me cool off. The next day, the staff sergeant wanted to see me. He put me in a room and left me there. I thought to myself, "What a weird way to release someone." When he came back, he started asking me a bunch of questions. I couldn't figure out what was going on. I kept asking him why. What are all the questions about? Then he told me.

"Two of his officers had been practicing with the drug dogs when they got a scent from my car. On further inspection, they found a kilo of cocaine in the right rear door. Then he arrested me. He said I'd have to stay in jail at least until Monday.

"They took my fingerprints and picture and put me back in the cell." Jessie was wringing her hands, not looking at him.

"Saturday morning, Jones came back. They were unable to match my prints with those found on the door panel or the drugs. He released me, telling me I had to stay in town, that they would be keeping my car as evidence. The officer who had originally arrested me brought me here." As she finished her story, she finally looked at him, expecting to see disbelief or cynicism.

Instead, Dave looked at her with compassion. When she saw that, she slumped into a chair across from where he sat and waited for him to speak.

"Wow," was all he said at first.

A few minutes later he added, "There's got to be more to this Jessie. What haven't you told me?"

She leaned back in her chair and stared up at the ceiling. "I don't know much else. I've been trying to figure out how all this happened. You've got to believe me Dave; this is not my type of thing. I hate drugs and anything to do with them."

"I believe what you say Jessie, but someone had to put the bag there in the first place. Who could it be? Have you talked to everyone you know?"

"Yes, I've done that," she said, evading his question of who it could have been. "I'm at my wit's end. It was such a relief to talk to Aunt Mae today. You were right, she makes it seem like everything will be all right."

"You should go out and stay with her," he suggested. "It would do you good."

"I wanted to, but the staff sergeant said I had to stay here for now." Jessie stood and slowly walked to the window. "Thanks for listening, Dave. It helps just to talk to someone about this. I didn't want to burden Aunt Mae with this."

Dave walked up behind her and put his hands on her shoulders to turn her around to face him. "I can't help feeling that there's more to this that you're not telling me. I'll talk to Jones later and see if there's anything that he's not telling you. It's going to be okay, Jessie." He folded her into his arms and held her close.

Jessie put her arms around his waist and sighed. It felt so good; it was nice to have some physical comfort. They stayed that way for several minutes. Soon though, her heartbeat quickened and she could feel his pick up the pace as well. She leaned back and looked up at him only to find him watching her, a lazy, hazy look in his eyes. Slowly, as if they were pulled together by a spider's web, their heads inched closer together. The first touch of their lips was soft and sweet but before long hunger and passion took over, making them breathless.

Finally, they broke it off. Jessie stepped away and held the back of her hand against her swollen lips.

"Oh my god," Dave managed.

Jessie blushed; she was shy all of a sudden. She looked up at him through lowered lashes. "I knew it," she whispered.

"You knew what?"

"Oh! I, I didn't mean to speak out loud," she stammered. "I, uh, I've got to go. Bye." She fled back to her room.

CHAPTER THIRTY

B RANT NEEDED TO find a way to get out of this house again.

Domer hadn't come home the night before, which didn't really matter all that much to him. He'd been woken up that morning by the noise of someone banging on the front door. He'd gotten off the couch as fast as his aching muscles would allow so he could look out the window where he saw two cops standing on the porch. Suddenly his muscles worked just fine and he made a beeline for the kitchen, almost knocking Susie over in his haste.

He waited just inside the kitchen so he could hear what the cops wanted; afraid they knew all about him, that Jessie had spilled the beans anyway. He stole a quick look in the living room and saw his blood-soaked shirt and jacket where he'd left them the night before. Hopefully, no one would notice.

A gasping scream brought his attention back to the front door. Susie had collapsed against one of the officers, her eyes wide with shock, her expression one of disbelief. Brant strained to listen to her babble and finally made out her words.

"Oh no, oh no, JD's not dead, not dead, can't be," she was saying over and over.

Brant stumbled backward and just managed to stop himself from falling to the floor. He grabbed the back of a chair and slowly sat down.

He must have been sitting there for quite a while because the next thing he noticed was that Stack and Dickie were talking about it in the kitchen, standing beside a pot full of coffee that hadn't been there earlier.

Brant got up and made his way to the living room, his only thought was to finish dressing and find Jessie.

He grabbed his jacket from the chair and silently made his way to the door. With one hand on the doorknob, he listened carefully. It sounded like Stack and

Dickie were in the middle of something. He looked outside. The car was gone, so that should mean that Mike wasn't around.

Careful to keep quiet, he eased the door open. So far, so good. With one last look toward the kitchen, Brant closed the door and stepped carefully down the steps, making sure to miss the loose one.

As soon as his feet hit the sidewalk, he took off at a run. When he turned the corner, he slowed down and then stopped to catch his breath.

On the move once again, he walked with his head down. If anyone saw his face, they'd just stare at him, and he didn't want to be noticed. Two blocks down the street, he saw a police cruiser drive by heading in the opposite direction. Brant foolishly turned to look, and then fear stopped him as his eyes locked with the officer's.

Brant quickly dragged his gaze away again, but by then it was too late. He heard the squeal of tires and then the sound of the siren. He put his head down again and started walking faster. The cruiser pulled up beside him and stopped. The officer jumped out and ran after him.

"Hold it right there!"

Brant looked back.

The officer was standing on the sidewalk, legs spread and arms stretched in front of him, his gun in his hands.

Brant stopped then, slowly, turned around, raising his hands.

"Put your hands behind your head and kneel on the ground," the officer ordered.

As soon as Brant complied, the officer relaxed his stance and came forward, his gun lowered but still in front.

Brant stared at the gun as it moved closer, beads of sweat glistening on his forehead and his hands slippery with it.

The gun stopped three feet in front of his face.

"All right, buddy, slowly take off your jacket."

Brant looked up in surprise, as if he hadn't known the cop was there, holding the gun. He inched the jacket off his shoulders and laid carefully it on the ground.

"Okay, now stand up and turn around."

He pulled himself up on shaky legs and concentrated on turning without falling, just managing it.

As soon as his back was turned his left arm was brought down and twisted behind his back, the action so fast that all he felt was the cuff going on. The move was repeated with his right arm. The officer pulled him to the car and stuffed him in the back seat.

The drive to the station was quiet. Brant was in shock, afraid to say anything in case he got into more trouble. How had they found out so fast? It must have been Jessie who told them. It couldn't be, though, they had agreed last night that he would look after everything himself. It was time for him to take responsibility. Jessie couldn't have known everything would change. Could she? His mouth opened and closed, over and over, involuntarily. If the cop were watching him, he'd see a beat-up young man who looked like a fish out of water, gasping for his last breath.

He was taken to an interrogation room. Coincidentally, it was the same one Jessie had been in only a few days before, but he had no way of knowing that. After what seemed an eternity, the door opened and a large man walked in.

"My name is Staff Sergeant Jones. What is your name?" He sat down across from Brant.

"Brant Lane, sir." If he'd had his wits about him he would have realized this was a strange question, assuming they already knew about him.

"Lane?" the staff sergeant asked.

"Yes," he replied.

"Any relation to Jessie Lane?"

"My sister," he mumbled.

Jones nodded his head. "Do you have any idea why you're here?" he asked.

Brant opened his mouth to answer, and then frowned, finally realizing he didn't really know what was going on.

"No, sir, I don't think I do," he said, his voice a little stronger.

Jones looked at him quizzically, clearly not believing him.

"Well, Mr. Lane, I have a few questions for you."

"What about?"

"There was an incident last night. Do you know what I'm referring to?"

"No."

"Really? Your face tells me another story. How did it happen?"

Brant looked down at his hands, folded on the table. "Got into a fight," he mumbled.

"What? I didn't hear you, boy."

He cleared his throat. "I got into a fight," he repeated.

"Who with?"

"I don't know." He looked up and saw skepticism on Jones's face. "Some guy," he added.

"Why?"

"I'd never seen him before."

"Not why didn't you know him, wiseass, but why did you get into a fight?"

"We had an argument."

"About what?"

"What's with all the questions? Am I under arrest or something? I didn't do anything wrong except get into a fight." He lowered his head again and moved his hands from the tabletop to the top of his legs where they moved back and forth of their own volition.

"I'll ask the questions here," Jones stated, as he got up and left the room.

Brant sat in the room, alone, for more than three hours. Every so often, Jones would come back in the room and ask the same questions again and again. Once in a while, he would add a few new ones, such as: who was the guy he fought with? What did he look like? How long did it last? Who won?

Every time a question was asked, Brant played dumb. He wasn't sure what was going on and until they told him, he had decided he wasn't going to say anything other than what had already been said.

Every time they left him alone, Brant got up and walked around. He looked at his face in the large mirror and felt his bruises, as if to remind him that all this was for real. Some of the puffiness had started to subside, but he was purple where Domer had hit him.

Again, the door opened and Jones walked in. This time he motioned for Brant to stand up. "Brant Lane, you are under arrest for the murder of John Domer."

Jones continued talking but Brant ceased to listen after he heard the word "murder." He was under arrest for murder!

Jones finished reading him his rights and then herded him to booking. There, his fingerprints and picture were taken. Brant finally snapped out of his shocked daze when the flashbulb went off.

"Hey, what about my phone call?" he demanded.

"You'll get it when we're done here," Jones responded.

Two more pictures were snapped, he was allowed to wash the ink off his hands, and then he was finally allowed to make his call.

"Hello," she answered.

"Jessie?"

"Brant? Is that you? What's wrong? Where are you?"

"Jessie, I'm in jail," he whispered into the phone. "Jessie, they think I killed Domer!"

CHAPTER THIRTY-ONE

JESSIE CAREFULLY SET the phone back on its cradle. Brant arrested for murdering John? It couldn't be possible.

Could it?

She thought about their meeting the night before: Brant, beaten and shaken, scared out of his mind. Had he told her everything? When he mentioned Stack and Dickie, she had wanted to ask him who they were but by the time he'd calmed down enough to really talk, he'd left.

Brant was in over his head, that much was obvious. Had he lost all control and killed John? It didn't seem possible, but then, none of this would have seemed possible only a week ago.

She stopped herself. Had it really only been one week? Seven days? Is that all it took to completely change a person's life?

She had left home Wednesday afternoon and drove straight through, only stopping for gas and a couple of hours of sleep when exhaustion had forced her to. Late on Thursday, she had been stopped by the RCMP and had ended up in jail. On Friday she found out there were drugs hidden in her car and she would probably have to stay in jail until Monday. Saturday, she was released and taken to the motel where she met Dave, and then they later had dinner. She smiled to herself at that memory.

Sunday, the previous day, she had explored Poplar Grove and had tried to call some of Brant's friends; she had finally reached them that afternoon. Brant himself had called her not long after that, saying he was in Poplar Grove. She still didn't really know how he'd found her.

After her argument with Dave, she had gone out, then met Domer and ended up going out for dinner with him. And now here she was, it was Monday, and the only really good thing to happen so far this day was reuniting with Aunt Mae.

She groaned as she realized that she hadn't been gone even a full week and her life was in ruins. Or was it? It was true, this wasn't exactly what she had planned as a way to sort things out, but at least Brant was safe in jail.

It would be nice to have some time to sort through her feelings about Dave. The time they had spent together so far had been electrifying for her. She struggled to ignore the voice in her head telling her that he couldn't be trusted. She hadn't heard that voice in a very long time but the argument she'd had with Linda seemed to bring back her deepest fears. The fear that she didn't deserve to love anyone and have them love her back; the fear that if she trusted anyone, they'd only let her down.

Now was not the time; she shook her head in an attempt to push those thoughts aside. She grabbed her jacket and headed for the police station.

Just inside the detachment door she stopped and looked around. It looked quite different from this view. If it wasn't for Brant, she wouldn't have seen it from any perspective, she thought to herself, conveniently forgetting the part she had played at the beginning of it all.

In front of her was a long counter stretching across half of the room. Behind it sat an officer. To the right and behind the counter were eight desks, some of which were occupied. Jessie walked up to the counter.

"Excuse me, sir."

The officer looked up at her. "Yeah, what can I do for you?" he asked, a bored look on his face.

"I'd like to see my brother, Brant Lane." She looked around as if she hoped to find him in the room.

"Well, I don't know if I can do that," was the reply. "Hang on." He pulled himself out of the chair and wandered to an office at the back of the room. A few minutes later he came back with the staff sergeant following him.

"Ms. Lane, I hear you'd like to see your brother." It was a statement not a question.

"Yes, sir, Staff Sergeant, I would appreciate it," she replied meekly, finding it hard to look him in the eyes.

"Have you arranged counsel for him?" Jones asked.

"No. I need to talk to him first. May I?" Jessie went out of her way to be polite; she didn't want to find herself on the wrong side of a cell door again.

"Yeah, all right. Follow me."

He led her through the maze of desks to an interrogation room. With a shiver, she entered. Jones left the door open while he went to get Brant.

"Jessie!" Brant ran the last few steps to her then enveloped her in a bear hug. Jessie squeezed back, and they both sat down.

"Brant, what's going on? What are you doing here? Did you tell them anything?" Jessie leaned toward him and put a hand on his shoulder. He sat with his head in his hands.

"I didn't do it, Jessie, I swear." He looked up then; his eyes were wet with tears. "You've gotta believe me, sis," he pleaded.

"Before I can do that you have to tell me everything. I mean everything this time, Brant. I have a feeling you left out a lot of the details before."

The door to the room they were in had been left open, so Brant moved his chair next to Jessie so he could bend his head near hers; that way the chance of anyone listening was remote.

"Okay, Jessie, I'll tell you everything," he whispered. "It pretty much all started with the drugs. Well, sort of," he amended.

Jessie scowled at him. "Spill it," she ordered.

"Okay, okay. It started a few months ago. I had started betting again . . ."

"Brant! I thought you'd left all that behind!" she interrupted.

"Quiet!" he admonished her. "You can't get loud every time I tell you something you don't like or I can't tell you any more, understand?"

"Yeah, yeah. Just get on with it."

"Okay. You can give me shit later, just chill out for now." He then told her the story of how he got to Poplar Grove. "There's something going on here though. Stack has been meeting someone here, and I get the feeling something is brewing. I don't know what, but I just have a feeling it isn't good."

Jessie sat still for a few minutes and tried to absorb it all. The background noise of the detachment slowly filtered into her hearing. She hadn't realized that she had ceased to hear it until she heard it again.

"Let me get a couple things straight," she whispered to Brant. "You mean to tell me you owed this Stack person money so you stole his own drugs from him and then tried to sell them back to him?" Brant nodded. "Are you nuts?"

"Yeah, okay, it wasn't the smartest thing to do, but I didn't know Dickie worked for Stack, how could I? Now look where it's gotten me?"

"I hate to say this, Brant, but this is probably the best place for you." She could see he was going to protest. "No, I mean it. All your life I've bailed you out, but not this time. I'll do what I can to help, of course, but you're going to have to pay for your mistakes." Jessie put her arm around him and squeezed lightly in reassurance.

"I know. I just can't believe they're going to hang Domer's murder on me." He used his hands to smooth back his hair, wincing when he accidentally touched a sore spot.

"How did that happen anyway? Why do they suspect you?"

"They have a witness who saw us fighting in the alley. The person 'viewed' me while I was being interrogated." He shrugged. "That we had a fight is true, but I didn't kill him."

She tapped her finger against her teeth as she thought again about what he had said. "I believe you," she finally said. "Tell me more about Stack and Dickie. You haven't really said very much about who they are."

Brant looked out through the doorway and watched as officers went about their business while he gathered his thoughts. "Stack is into a lot of things. Betting, drugs, prostitution; you name it. He's an all-round bad guy. Dickie, it turns out, is one of his henchmen. He's got his own stuff going on but his main thing is with Stack. Domer used to work for Stack but then something happened. From what I can figure out, he ripped Stack off somehow and then left town. It turns out that he came here. It was sheer chance that Dickie spilled the beans on that one."

Jessie was still tapping her finger. "So it seems as though John had some enemies. Maybe one of them killed him. I think I may have to start asking some questions just to see what I can find out." She paused for thought for a moment. "You should request a lawyer. I can't afford one for you and you don't have any money. You'll end up with one of those public defenders, but I don't see any way around it."

"Yeah, I guess you're right." He took her hand in his. "Jessie, I'm really sorry I got you involved in this mess. If I could do it all over again, things would be different." He looked at her with a twinkle, "I'd have found a different hiding place!"

"Brant! This is no time to joke."

"I had to break the mood," he looked at her from under slightly hooded eyes, this time his expression more appropriately a mixture of sorrow and helplessness that was hard to see amongst the bruises and swelling.

"I know," she commiserated as she patted his hand. "I'm going to leave now and see what I can find out." She pulled him into a hug. "I'll try to come and see you again tomorrow."

"Be careful, Jessie. I don't know what I'd do if something were to happen to you." He didn't want to let her go but eventually he loosened his grip.

Just then a guard walked in and pulled Brant from the room. Jessie waved to him as he was pulled around the corner and out of sight.

Now she had somewhere to start; she would find Stack and Dickie and see what information she could get.

CHAPTER THIRTY-TWO

JESSIE WANDERED AROUND town as she tried to come up with a plan of action. She knew the area where Brant had been staying but she didn't know the exact location; she decided to head in that general direction.

As she walked along she couldn't help but think about Brant. Even though he had caused her a lot of grief over the years he was still her favorite sibling. She smiled as she remembered the first time she had bailed him out.

He was in the fifth grade at the time. Jessie had been walking home from school and Brant came racing past her, looking over his shoulder every few steps. Jessie turned around to see what he was looking at but she couldn't see anything. She ran to catch up with him so she could find out what was up.

"What's the rush?" she asked him.

He couldn't keep still; he kept looking around her; he hopped from one foot to the other and back again. "There're some kids after me," he said, trying to catch his breath.

"Why?"

"They're mad at me. Can we keep going please?"

"Okay, but you need to tell me why they are mad at you." She had to grab onto his jacket to keep him from running off on her.

He looked up at her and you could see he was trying to decide whether she was trustworthy or not, whether or not she would tell on him. But she kept looking at him until he caved. It came out in a rush.

"I bet Joey I could beat him at marbles. He didn't believe me so we played." He shrugged. "I won so I took his favorite marble as my prize. Now he's mad at me. Him and some of the other boys said they was going to beat me up unless I gave it back." He watched her out of the corner of his eyes to see if she believed him or not. "I stuck my tongue out at them and then I ran away!"

Jessie laughed. "So now what are you going to do?"

"Well . . . I thought I'd give it back to him tomorrow." He hesitated. "I kind of did something bad."

"Oh?" she prompted him.

"Well, Joey's a big show-off. He's always makin' fun of me 'cause I'm so short. When he wasn't looking, I pushed a couple of his marbles out of the circle." He shrugged again. "I prob'ly wouldn't've won if I hadn't done that. I think one of his friends saw me."

"Brant! That's cheating! You know it's wrong to cheat. We're going back there right now so you can give Joey back his marble."

"Oh, Jessie," he whined. "Are you going to tell Mom?"

"Not if you do as I tell you."

They headed back to the school and met Joey and his friends part way. Jessie watched while Brant gave back the marble and apologized for cheating. Then she warned Joey not to pick on Brant anymore and suggested they all forget the whole thing.

If only things were that simple now. How nice it would be if all she had to do was find Joey again so she could make this all go away.

Jessie became aware of her surroundings once more; she had wandered into the area where she had met with Brant the first time. Because she was so wrapped up in her memories, she hadn't noticed anything, both then and now. She hoped she hadn't gone too far already but sensed she hadn't. As she turned around to get her bearings, she failed to notice that someone quickly ducked behind a parked car a block behind her.

She continued down the street, paying closer attention to the houses as she went, trying to spot something that resembled what Brant had described to her. The problem was that all the houses in this neighborhood all resembled each other in some way or another.

Two houses ahead she noticed a house that looked like it might fit the description Brant gave her; the grass was dead, the steps leading to the front door had seen much better days and there was a fancy car in the driveway. As she got closer, she looked at the plates: Ontario. It had to be the right house – how many people in this town would have people visiting from Ontario?

She had been so intent on finding the house that she hadn't really thought much further than that. What was she supposed to do now? She had to come up with something quickly since she couldn't just stand there on the street. Nothing came to her so she decided to wing it.

She straightened her back, squared her shoulders, shook her head to clear her mind and carefully mounted the rickety stairs.

The sound her knock made surprised her with its strength. The young woman who answered the door was another surprise.

"Can I help you?" she asked timidly.

"Uh, yes. Is there someone here named Stack?"

The young woman nodded, sniffled and motioned for her to enter.

Jessie followed her to the living room where she was told to wait. She took in her surroundings: ratty furniture and mismatched curtains. In spite of that, though, the room was spotlessly clean.

"Who are you?"

The question startled her and caused her gasp as she turned around. There were two men standing there, kind of the all male version of Ma and Pa Kettle, one short and slim, the other one large and tall.

"Jessie, my name is Jessie."

"What do you want?" asked the large one.

"I'm, um, I'm looking for someone named Stack."

"Well, you found him," the short one answered.

Jessie stared at him. So this was the man that Brant was involved with. He did look kind of mean and unforgiving.

"I asked you what you want." He looked at her with cold eyes that showed none of the curiosity he was feeling.

"I'm here about Brant." She returned his stare, her uncertainty visible.

"What about him? He's not here right now." He looked at her closely. "Who did you say you were again?" He didn't want her to know how important she had been to him.

"My name is Jessie." She cleared her throat. "Brant is my brother."

Stack walked over and stopped a foot in front of her. He looked up and down her body, which made her skin crawl so badly that she wanted to cover herself, but she fought to stay in control.

"So you're the famous sister," he drawled. "Look at this, Dickie, this is what's caused us so much trouble. Can you believe it?"

Dickie laughed gruffly. "No, boss, I sure can't!"

"Where's my stuff?" Stack demanded.

"The cops have it," she responded. She felt her spine stiffen as her body fought the fear that was threatening to overtake her.

"What are you doing here, then? If you don't have my stuff, why are you here?" He thrust his face at her. Then he smiled. "Oh, you must be here to pay me my money instead, right?"

"No," she croaked out, took a deep breath, and then plunged ahead. "I came here to find out what's going on."

Stack stared at her for a second before he laughed at her. Dickie was quick to join him.

"What makes you think I'll say anything to you?" Stack responded as soon as he could catch his breath. "Maybe we'll keep you here and give that brother of yours a reason to pay me back." Then he grabbed her arm in a steely grip and yanked her toward him. "What do you think about that?"

She gasped at the pain in her arm, and he squeezed it a few more times before he let her go, though he clearly enjoyed himself and was loath to stop. She rubbed at the soreness in her arm and watched him through tear-filled eyes. "Lot of good it would do you since Brant's in jail." She took some satisfaction in the quick look of surprise that crossed his face at her news.

"What did you say?"

"I said that Brant is in jail. Now I want to know what the hell is going on here," she demanded, strength filling her voice with every word. "Did you kill John and frame Brant for it?"

Stack shook his head and looked at her quizzically. "Who the fuck is John?"

"Uh, boss, she means Domer, I think," Dickie cut in.

"What? Oh, JD, yeah." Stack turned away to think and took a few steps around the room. "So the cops think Lane did it, eh? Isn't that an interesting turn of events." He turned back toward Jessie. "I don't know anything about that. I didn't think the little shit had it in him, I really didn't."

"He didn't do it, I tell you!" Could she be wrong in thinking that Stack had done it?

"And you think I know who did it? And that I'd tell you?"

"Well, you weren't getting anywhere with him. Why not get him out of the way?"

"If I wanted him out of the way missy, I'd've just had him killed. How the hell would I get my money back? Don't be stupid." He walked over to a chair and sat down.

"There's something else going on here. What is it?" She had no idea where the thought had come from but now that it was out there, it made sense. This guy had sure gone to a lot of trouble for what had to be a relatively small amount of cocaine in his operation.

His fixed her with his narrowed stare. "What do you know about that?" he demanded as he pushed off the chair and came back at her again. "Who's been talking to you?"

Jessie backed up, visibly shaken. "Nothing, no one, I swear." She held up her hands. "Forget I said anything." Maybe it was time for her to give it a break for now. She had rattled his cage, that much was obvious, but she was getting a bad feeling about all of this. It was time to get away so she could regroup and think about what she'd learned.

"I'm going to leave now," she announced. "But let me just warn you. I don't know what's going on here but I will find out, somehow, and when I do, you're going to pay for everything you've done."

By the time she had finished her short speech she was at the door, which she opened quickly and fled.

Stack watched the door bang shut and then stalked into the kitchen.

"Did you hear all of that?" he demanded. He was talking to the person who had been sitting hidden in the kitchen the whole time.

"Yes, I did. Now do you believe me when I say she's got to go? It may have been dumb luck that gave you an excuse to come out here, but you know we've got to finish what we started. I've waited too long for this to have it all spoiled by some goody-two-shoes like her."

"And what do you suggest we do? Huh? We don't want to draw any undue attention on ourselves, it's too risky." Stack grabbed a beer for himself and sat at the table. "Dickie, make yourself useful and grab something for our guest."

Dickie pushed away from the doorway and did as he was told.

"Someone I know owes me. I'll take care of it. Don't bother with a drink for me, thanks. I have to leave now."

Stack watched the guest leave by the back door, careful to avoid being seen by anyone in the neighborhood. He watched as the car headed down the back alley before he turned back to Dickie.

"That is one cold-hearted woman," he said with a smile on his face. "It's too bad we're only here for a short while. I'd like to get to know her better, if you know what I mean."

The object of his desire was well aware of what he wanted, but Claire Hyde was meant for one man and one man only.

That man was Dave Sterling.

CHAPTER THIRTY-THREE

JESSIE DIDN'T SLOW down until she was two blocks away. She had a feeling Stack wouldn't pay much attention to her threat. Who was she anyway? Just someone mixed up in something that was way beyond her ability to deal with. If it wasn't for Brant . . . well, if it wasn't for Brant, she wouldn't be in this mess.

She stopped to take a look around, to give herself a minute or two to catch her breath and slow her racing heart. There was an inviting patch of green grass beneath a poplar tree so she plunked herself down and hugged her knees to her chest.

If it weren't for Brant, she would be with Aunt Mae right at that very moment. Jessie smiled as she daydreamed about what they'd be doing. They'd be talking about all sorts of things, she imagined. If only she could be there right now!

Jessie got back on her feet; as she told herself to quit feeling sorry for herself she headed back to the motel.

She had almost reached the so-called downtown area when she thought she heard a scraping noise. It was out of place so she stopped to listen. Everything was quiet, so she continued on. The noise came again a few seconds later but this time she didn't stop. It sounded like something was being dragged along the ground. Her heart began a heavy thud in her chest. She tried to pick out the sound over her heartbeat; it sounded like a stick being dragged. That seemed silly, so she convinced herself she was hearing things.

Without warning, Jessie was pushed to the ground from behind. She barely had enough time to push her arms out to block her fall. Before she could roll over and see what was happening, she felt a kick to her stomach that drove the air from her lungs. She doubled over and another kick landed on her ribs. She felt a sharp stab of pain in her side; her head was swimming with the pain, her eyes shut tight in concentration, her breathing labored.

It wasn't over yet.

Just as she caught her breath, she heard, rather than felt, the blow that landed on the back of her head – then, mercifully, nothing.

CHAPTER THIRTY-FOUR

Dave had finally finished weeding the flower garden. He sat back on his heels and surveyed his handiwork; Mae would be happy now. He checked his watch, it was after six o'clock, time to finish up the office work for the day and then see if he could talk to Jessie. He had stayed away from her since their kiss the night before; he didn't want her to know how much it had affected him.

It had been such a long time since he had been attracted to someone – not since Beth had died. When he first met Jessie he knew there was something special about her. He was just getting to know her when he found out about the drugs. He couldn't believe how wrong he was! Then, last night, when she told him about her brother, the relief it had brought to him had shocked him. It had only been a year since his wife and daughter had died; it was much too soon to be thinking about another woman. But no matter how often he told himself that, he just couldn't help it. There was something about Jessie that intrigued him. Maybe he felt sorry for her. No, that wasn't right, there was more to it than that.

Now he had to find her, he had to talk to her for a while. The last time he'd seen her she was walking toward downtown and that was a few hours earlier. She should be back by now, he estimated. He put his account books away and took a last look around his office to make sure everything was put away as it should be. Satisfied, he turned off the light and locked the door.

As soon as he got to her room he noticed that the curtains were drawn. He knocked on the door and waited.

A minute later he knocked again. She must not be there, which was rather odd, because he had noticed over the last couple of days that she would take a walk after lunch, but that she was normally back before long. Maybe something had happened to her?

As soon as the thought entered his mind, he was filled with a sense of foreboding. He jogged over to his truck and got in, determined to drive around and find her.

He slowly made his way down the streets of the downtown area, which caused other drivers to honk in frustration. He would pull over and let them pass, but he was not going to rush as he looked everywhere for Jessie. Because the downtown was so small, this part of his search only took fifteen minutes.

Next he headed for the nicer residential area.

When that search turned up nothing, he headed for the rougher neighborhood.

He was idling slowly down the street when he thought he saw something suspicious up ahead. It looked like someone was lying on the sidewalk. He sped up and pulled over to the curb. There was a body lying there.

He quickly slammed the truck into park and got out. He ran over to the body. "Oh my god, Jessie!" he whispered.

She was unconscious, blood pooling under her head.

He knelt down beside her and quickly felt along her neck and spine, checking for any breaks or swelling. Except for the head wound, she didn't seem too badly hurt. Her breaths were fast and shallow, and she was cool to touch. He had to get her to the hospital; she was in shock.

He ran to his truck and opened the tailgate, and then he grabbed an old blanket he kept behind the seat and laid it out on the truck bed to put her on. Being careful not to jar her, he picked her up and carefully carried her to the back of the truck. He set her on the blanket, then closed the tailgate and ran to the driver's seat.

Twenty minutes later, he pulled up in front of the small country hospital and yelled for help.

CHAPTER THIRTY-FIVE

DAVE WALKED THE hallway that led to the emergency room. It was a typical country hospital and it had only two floors. The reception area and emergency room shared the front of the building on the main floor. The rear half was used as a maternity ward, and it also housed the x-ray equipment and an emergency surgery suite. The cafeteria and laundry were in the basement. The second floor was used for all other patients.

Dave was impatient; Jessie had been in emergency for two hours already. The police had been called and had arrived only half an hour earlier. Dave had given his statement, which had been understandably sketchy.

He sat on an uncomfortable plastic chair, only to get up again and head down the short hall. On his return trip, the doctor finally came out. Dave quickened his pace so that he was almost running by the time they met.

"Doc, how is she? Is she okay?"

"Dave, she'll be okay." The doctor put a hand on his arm to try and calm him. "The ribs on her left side are badly bruised, as are her buttocks. She needed ten stitches to close the wound to her head but she doesn't have a skull fracture, thank God. She does have a concussion though, and we want her to stay overnight for observation."

Dave drew in a deep, soothing, calming breath. "Is she awake? Can I see her?"

The doctor nodded. "She's starting to come around now. You can go in for a few minutes." He held Dave's arm to stop him from running in right away. "She'll be a bit groggy, so be quiet, okay?"

"Yeah, okay, whatever you say," he responded as he walked away.

Jessie slowly became aware of her surroundings. When she tried to lift her head a sharp stab of pain stopped her; it felt like a migraine times five. She lay there and waited for the pain to subside. Just as it had become a dull ache she heard a scuffling noise. Startled, she turned her head quickly in that direction, which caused another jolt of pain to run across her head, which made her moan. She closed her eyes and waited once more for the pain to subside. It took longer this time before she could open her eyes again. When she did, Dave was standing beside her bed, a frown on his face.

"What's wrong?" she managed to croak. "I need a drink of water."

"What do you mean, 'what's wrong'?" Dave tried to whisper due to her head injury and pain, but the emotion in his voice made it difficult. "Are you okay? How do you feel?"

"You're frowning."

"What?" As soon as he realized what she meant, he worked hard to relax his facial muscles. "Is this better?" He had tried to smile but that just wasn't going to happen.

"Yes." She tried to make her lips form a smile but couldn't. "I feel like someone used my head for a basketball," she told him.

"You had me worried," he murmured, as he leaned over and brushed her hair away from her face. "Do you remember what happened to you?"

Jessie started to shake her head but quickly stopped when the pain hit again. "No, not really."

"The staff sergeant is waiting to talk to you. Do you feel up to it?"

"I may as well get it over with." She tried to sit up but couldn't move without a lot of pain. "I still need that drink of water."

"I'll get it for you." He walked over and parted the curtain that was closed around her bed. Jones was waiting for him. Dave held his hand up to halt Jones while he went and got Jessie's water. Jones followed him back to Jessie's bed.

"Hi, Jessie," Jones said as he approached her.

Jessie winced at the sound of his voice; he had spoken in a normal conversational tone, but to her it was as if he had yelled at her from across the room.

"You need to whisper," Dave reminded him. "She's been banged on the head among other things." He helped her take a sip of water.

"Sorry," Jones whispered. "Doc Schaefer did tell me about her injuries. I'm sorry, Jessie." He walked up to stand right beside the bed and leaned over slightly so she could hear him easier. "You don't look very good, Jessie. Do you remember anything about what happened?"

"Not really." She tried to concentrate and remember but the throbbing in her head made her stop. "I can't remember much," she finally managed. "I was walking and then I heard a noise. I think I stopped, I'm not sure, and then I think someone pushed me. I don't remember anything else. I'm sorry."

"Don't apologize, you've done real well," Jones was quick to reassure her. "You may remember more when the pain in your head subsides. Do you have any idea who would do this to you?"

"I don't know. When can I get out of here?" She tried again to lift herself and managed a few inches before collapsing.

"The doc says you need to stay here tonight," Jones told her. "They want to keep an eye on you, on account of your head injury."

"Okay, Jones," Dave cut in. "I think she's had enough for now. She needs some more rest." He ushered the officer out to the hallway.

By the time he returned to Jessie, she was asleep. He sat down on the small chair beside the bed and kept watch. Even with some of her hair shaved off and an ugly bruise on her forehead, she was quite beautiful in a peaceful sort of way. This was the first time he had allowed himself to really think about what had happened. Earlier, he had been just plain worried about her well-being. Now that she was going to be all right, he took the opportunity to examine his feelings.

When he had realized it was Jessie lying on that sidewalk, his mind had frozen and instinct took over.

Now he wondered why this had happened. What had she been up to? He didn't want to believe that she really was mixed up in the whole drug thing but he couldn't just discount it out of hand. The disappointment he was feeling was like a yoke on his shoulders. He shrugged it off. He wouldn't just jump to conclusions; he had done that before with her and they had fallen out over it.

The feelings of protectiveness and concern were overwhelming him, and he had a hard time believing that he could feel like that, to this degree at any rate, for just anyone. He couldn't ignore the relief he'd felt when she had spoken to him, the relief he saw in her eyes when she saw him.

"What time is it?"

Startled out of his musings, he quickly sat up and leaned toward her. "It's almost eleven. How do you feel?" He put his hand on hers.

"I still have a monster headache." She tried to lick her lips, to give them some moisture. "My mouth is dry, is there any more of that water?"

"Yes," he answered. "While you were asleep, the nurse brought in a pitcher of ice water. Maybe you'd like a piece of ice first?"

"Thanks, yes," she said, opening her mouth.

While she sucked on the piece of ice, he slipped out and got the nurse.

"Well now, how are we feeling?" the nurse asked.

"I've got a splitting headache and it hurts to breathe," Jessie answered, her voice sounding a little like sandpaper.

"The doctor left instructions for a pain killer. Can you sit up?"

"I think so." She began to move; she winced at her achy muscles and throbbing head but she managed to prop herself in a semi-sitting position. The nurse handed her a pill and the glass of water Dave had filled for her. Jessie took the pill and leaned back to rest.

"That should start to work in ten minutes or so," the nurse told her and then she turned to Dave. "We're getting a room ready for her upstairs; it shouldn't be too long now."

"Thanks, Julie," Dave responded as she left them alone once again. "How are you feeling now?" he asked Jessie.

"Like I want to get out of here," she answered.

"You're crazy. Doc Schaefer said you should stay here tonight. You've got a severe blow to the head and you need to be watched."

"Please Dave," she pleaded. "I hate hospitals. Please take me back to the motel. I'll be okay, I promise."

"No, Jessie, you have to stay here."

She struggled to sit higher on the bed. The effort left her gasping with pain, which in turn aggravated her bruised ribs. She took a few minutes to slow down her breathing to ease the pain.

"Look, Dave. Something's going on around here. My getting beat up proves that. I need to find out what's happening and I can't do that from here. I'll get a much better rest where I feel comfortable." She looked up at him, begging him with her eyes.

It only took a few seconds.

"I'll go have a quick word with the doctor," he said, hoping the doctor would give him some ammunition to convince her she had to stay put.

Ten minutes later, he came back to find Jessie sitting on the side of the bed with her legs hanging down.

"Boy, are you determined, or what?"

She frowned at him, quickly followed by a wince.

"Okay, okay. The doc says it's okay as long as you take the pills he's prescribed for you." He waved the prescription at her. "I'll have to stay with you so I can wake you every hour just to make sure you don't lose consciousness." He watched her face carefully; it was easy to see the pain she was feeling. "I have to tell you Jessie, I don't know if this is the right thing to do. Look at you!"

She tried to scowl and when that hurt too much, she gave up and instead, asked, "Where are my clothes?"

"Are you sure you want to do this?"

Her look of determination answered for her.

He went to a little cupboard and got out a bag filled with her clothes and handed it to her.

"I don't know how good they'll be since they had to cut them off of you." He pulled her pants out of the bag and showed her where they had cut them. They looked like they were being made into maternity pants. "Hey, what are you doing?"

"What does it look like I'm doing? I'm getting up!" She had been inching her way off the bed, hanging on to the adjustable lamp neck like it was her lifeline. "Pass me the bag; I'll manage."

"Do you want some help? I could get Julie to give you a hand."

She waved him away, her arm making short, jerky movements by her side. "No, I'll be okay. Just stay close by, okay?"

Dave threw her a worried look and then did as he was told.

Twenty long minutes later, she called out to him.

He walked to her and had to bite his lip to stop from bursting out laughing. She had tied her shirt around her breasts and was trying to hold up her jeans with one hand.

"Don't you dare laugh at me," she scowled at him.

"Here, wear this." He smiled and draped his jacket over her shoulders.

With his arm around her for support, he walked her out to where a wheelchair was waiting. She eased herself into the chair with a sigh of relief.

When they reached his truck, she was determined to get in all by herself. After three tries to lift her leg into the cab, she finally gave up and let him lift her in. When he tried to change her mind about leaving, she ignored him.

He pulled in the motel parking lot and coasted up to her door then gently stopped the truck. He looked over at her. Her eyes were closed, so he assumed she was asleep.

"Jess?"

"I'm awake," she groaned. "Did you have to hit every bump in the road?"

"I did the best I could. Do you want me to take you back to the hospital?"

"No! Would you just come and help me out of this torture chamber and into my room?"

He got out of the truck and went around to the passenger side.

Jessie had to work to pry her fingers from the door armrest. When he opened the door, she slowly turned her body so she could slide off the seat. Dave could see she was having problems so he just reached in and scooped her in his arms.

If I weren't in such pain I'd really enjoy this, thought Jessie.

He carried her up the steps and then gently set her on her feet. She leaned against the wall while he grabbed his keys out of his pocket. As soon as the door was open, he helped her walk over to the bed and then eased her down so she was sitting on it.

"Will you be okay here for a few minutes?" he asked. "I just want to go to my place and get a blanket and some pillows."

"Help me to the bathroom first, please. I'll try to be in bed by the time you get back."

He could see that she was in considerable pain, but when he suggested she take a breather until he came back, she became agitated. He got her another pain pill just before he walked her to the bathroom.

It only took a couple of minutes for him to get what he needed from his place, but he waited outside until he saw the bathroom door start to open before he went back into Jessie's room. He helped her get in bed and tucked the blankets around her and made sure she was as comfortable as she could be. Then he set about seeing to his own bed and comfort.

By the time he was set up, she was fast asleep. He knew it would be a long time before he would be able to sleep, but he set his alarm for the first wake-up anyway, just in case. Beside Jessie's bed, he bent over her and placed a gentle kiss on the nonbruised side of her forehead.

She smiled in her sleep.

CHAPTER THIRTY-SIX

IT WAS A long night. Dave didn't rely on his alarm at all and woke Jessie every hour. Once in a while she would cry out in her sleep but as soon as he touched her shoulder she would quiet down again. By seven he couldn't keep his eyes open so he set his alarm for the eight o'clock wake up.

When he woke up, it was almost noon and Jessie was moving around the room.

"Oh my god, I overslept the alarm!" He jumped up to check on Jessie. "I'm so sorry, are you okay, Jessie?"

"I'm sore as hell but at least my head feels a little better. You were so deeply asleep that I didn't want to wake you up." She made her way over to the couch, stopping only once to catch her breath, and settled on the arm. She lifted her hand to touch her head. "I can't believe they had to shave part of my head. Does it look really awful? I couldn't really see." The blow to her head had landed just below the top of head toward the back.

"No," he reassured her, "you can hardly see it and your hair covers it up nicely." He folded his blanket and picked up his pillow. "Have you eaten anything yet?"

"No. I was feeling nauseous when I woke up so I didn't want to chance it. I'm better now and hungry. Why? Are you going to make me breakfast?" She looked up at him with a smile on her face.

"Yes, I think I will." He grabbed his blanket. "I'll make scrambled eggs. How does that sound?"

"It sounds wonderful, Dave, but I was only kidding. I should be cooking for you after all you've done for me."

"No, you just sit and relax. I'll be back in a jiffy."

He was gone before she could protest any further.

He was back again half an hour later with a tray of eggs, toast and juice. Jessie was seated at the small table, with her hands cradling her head and her elbows leaning on the table. She didn't seem to notice that he was back in the room.

"Jessie, are you okay?" he asked worriedly.

"Yes, I'm okay," she replied, "just resting and thinking." Slowly she raised her head. "That smells great."

Dave took a moment to look at her closely and what he saw dismayed him. Part of her forehead was scraped and the bruise under it was dark and ugly. Her eyes seemed sunken and bruised as well. He quickly set the tray down and reached out to take her chin in his hand.

"Are you really sure you're okay, Jessie?" On an even closer inspection, he noticed her eyes were dark from lack of sleep, not bruised. He softly touched the abrasion on her forehead. "Does this hurt?" he asked softly.

"It's not too bad. Do I really look that horrible?" she asked, a small frown creasing the part of her forehead that could move.

"No, it's not bad, it just looks sore." He unloaded their breakfast from the tray and sat down across from her. "Dig in before it gets too cold."

They ate without talking, each one busy with their own thoughts. When they were done, Dave stacked the dishes back on the tray. "Would you like some coffee now?" he asked her.

"Oh, yes, that would be perfect, Dave, thanks." She smiled at him weakly. She was feeling tired again but fought it.

"I put some on while I made breakfast so it should be ready. I'll just run these dishes over and bring back the coffee. You like yours black, right?"

"Yes," she agreed, flattered that he had remembered.

By the time he got back with the coffee, Jessie had managed to get to the couch. Dave handed her a mug of coffee and sat down in the nearby comfortable chair.

"Do you remember anything more about what happened Jessie?" he asked. Obviously she had been thinking about it so he thought they might as well talk about it.

"I don't remember a lot. I guess it was just a mugging. They got my purse so I'll have to report my credit cards stolen and all that."

"What do you mean 'they'?"

Jessie shrugged. "I don't know, just a figure of speech I guess. There was only one person that I know of."

This was new information. She hadn't been sure before now. He sat back and thought about what he knew, which wasn't much.

"It doesn't make sense," he finally said.

"What doesn't?" she asked.

"Robbery." He looked closely at her. "Why would someone beat you up so badly if the only motive was robbery? You've had all morning to think about this, was that the best you could come up with?"

Jessie just stared at him, defiance visible in her expression. There was also shock at his attack. "If I said I thought it was a mugging, that's what I believe."

"No, Jessie," he said, leaning forward in his chair. "I don't believe you. Here's what I know." He turned in the chair so he was facing her squarely. "You were arrested; they found drugs in your car but couldn't prove for sure that it was yours. They release you but you have to stay here. You meet some guy at a bar and now he's dead. You go for a walk and get beat up. Have I got it right so far?" He didn't realize how accusatory he sounded.

"Yes," she answered softly, her head lowered.

"And now you expect me to believe that last night was all about a mugging?" He shook his head in disbelief. "In a town where muggings don't normally happen? Think again."

He got up from his chair and moved to sit beside her on the couch. He picked up her hand and held it lightly in his own. "Jessie, I want to help you, but I can't if you won't tell me everything." His voice had finally softened.

Jessie looked at him, her eyes becoming watery with tears. She looked away. "I can't involve you, Dave . . ."

"Can't you see I'm involved already? Please look at me." He waited while she wiped her eyes with the back of her hand before looking at him. "I care about you, Jessie. Please let me help you." He reached over and took her other hand, turning her toward him.

She let out a small gasp of pain.

"Oh, I'm sorry," he said contritely. "Are you okay?"

"Yes," she smiled, "I'm okay, just no sudden movements, all right? Look, I've been thinking about this all morning. I can't make sense of everything that's happened. I do need help. I care about you too, but you've been through enough in the last year, I can't expect you to help me."

He stared at her in wonder and then frowned; there were things to think about, their feelings for each other could wait.

"Jessie, I want to help. I'm a big boy. I can make my own decisions. Now tell me what you know." Sitting with her like this, holding hands was becoming a strain for him. He let her go and got up to stand in front of the window and looked outside.

Jessie slowly pulled herself off the couch, wincing with the pain of her aching muscles, trying not to breathe too deeply. She walked over to the small table and sat down.

"Okay, Dave, I'll tell you." She was glad his back was turned but she lowered her head anyway, just in case he turned to look at her. "I mentioned my brother, Brant. Do you remember?"

"Yes, I remember."

"He's here, in Poplar Grove." She sensed that he had turned toward her again; she quickly looked up to confirm. "He's in jail now, arrested for murder. They think he murdered John Domer, but he didn't." She straightened her neck, lifted her head and looked him in the eye. "He may be guilty of a lot of things but murder isn't one of them." She stopped to catch her breath. "I'm getting ahead of myself.

"Since Brant was in high school, he's gotten into trouble gambling. I helped him out and made him promise never to bet again. He agreed. I thought everything was fine. That is until I arrived here, got arrested and they found the drugs he had stashed. Brant stole the cocaine from a man named Stack. He was going to sell them to someone he knew so that he could pay back the money that he owed. He stashed the drugs in my car for a day but I screwed everything up and left town before he had a chance to remove the bag."

"Wait a second, who did he owe money to?"

"Stack. Yes, I know it sounds strange but that was what Brant was going to do. Steal drugs from Stack, sell it, and give Stack the money."

Dave looked at her with awe. "That really took cojones – sorry, gumption – to pull off a stunt like that. Okay, so what happened next?"

"I may be a bit hazy on the details, but this is what I know: The guy Brant was going to sell the drugs to works for Stack; his name is Dickie. Dickie realizes that the drugs belong to Stack, so he sets Brant up by saying he was going to help him. They basically kidnap Brant and want him to lead them to me. The problem was that Brant didn't know where I'd gone. I don't know how they did it, but they did catch up to me here. I've met with Brant a couple of times, which is how I found out about him and the drugs. He told me about the place where they were holding him, and then yesterday morning Brant was arrested for murder. I went to see him in jail. He's not guilty, Dave, not of murder. I just know it." Telling this story had taken a lot out of her. She wrapped her arms around her stomach and let out a soft moan, then gasped with the pain.

Dave rushed over to her, then went to the bathroom and found the pills the doctor had prescribed for her. He handed her a pill and a glass of water and watched her as she took it. After a few minutes, she managed to slow her breathing enough to get up and slowly move about the room. When he was satisfied she would be okay, he thought over everything she had told him. Something still didn't jibe, but he couldn't put his finger on what.

"Okay, you've explained about the drugs, but that doesn't explain the rest of this," he motioned at her with his arm. "There's something missing. What aren't you telling me, Jessie?"

"Yes, there's something else going on, there has to be." She sat down on her chair again. "Why else would Stack stay here when there's no way for him to get his dope back? I've been trying to figure it out but I just can't seem to see it. Yesterday, Brant told me that Stack has been meeting with someone, but he didn't know who. At first, Brant thought Stack was meeting a woman, but he said that couldn't be, because Stack was never happier when he got back from these meetings than he was when he left, meaning, well, you know." She blushed. "Anyway, after I left Brant, I wandered around trying to figure it all out. I found myself in the really old part of town. I figured the only place to look would be with Stack himself. Brant had described the house and I knew I just had to find a car with Ontario plates. I found the house and car and so I went in to meet Stack. He wouldn't tell me anything so I left. I was on my way back here when I was attacked."

"Are you crazy? Going to see this guy on your own?" He shook his head. "Well, obviously, you've got someone worried." He walked over and put his arm on her shoulder. "Jessie, maybe you're just not seeing things as they really are. It sounds to me like your brother is a thief and a murderer. I know you don't think so, but this is the way I see it: he was taking the easy way out; he ripped off this Stack guy, John Domer must have known something Brant didn't want him to, so that's why he killed him."

Jessie pushed Dave's hand off her shoulder. "I can't believe that. Brant may be a lot of things but a murderer he is not! I asked for your help but for you to say that my brother is a murderer is not helping. It's my belief in him that's allowing me to try to help him. I can't abandon him, I can't!" Her breaths were labored, but the pain in her head and chest weren't quite so bad this time.

"Look, I'm sorry if I've upset you," Dave said. "But after all the trouble he's caused you, I don't understand why you're still defending him. I need to think." He left her room, closing the door none too softly behind him.

CHAPTER THIRTY-SEVEN

DAVE WAS IN his living room, moving from place to place, unable to settle anywhere specific. He just couldn't understand why Jessie was so adamant. Why would she put her trust in someone who was so obviously guilty?

He tried to look at things from her point of view. Brant was her brother; he had done some shady things and had pulled Jessie in as well. That alone convinced him that Brant was a liar and a user.

He replayed their conversation over in his mind, trying to come up with some ideas. One thing he had learned about Jessie: she was a very loyal person. But hadn't that loyalty gotten her into enough trouble?

The more he thought this over, the more it bothered him. Something seemed very familiar about the events of the last few days.

Why was he so quick to question Jessie's belief when he was so positive his family had been murdered? No one else thought so but he had seen the road marks. He knew Beth, knew what kind of driver she was.

He finally collapsed on the couch.

No one believed him. He remembered how alone that had made him feel at the time; it still did, if he was perfectly honest with himself. Did he really want Jessie to feel the way he did?

And what about his own family? What if it were one of his siblings?

Again, he went over everything he knew. The secret meetings involving that man, Stack, bothered him. Who was he meeting with? Did it have something to do with drugs?

He went over everything that had happened, the people around town he'd talked to. He remembered seeing Jack Enders a few days earlier. He'd seemed distracted and when Dave had asked him about it, Enders was rude to him; it wasn't like him at all. Dave counted Enders as one of the few friends he had in Poplar Grove. Later, he heard that Enders had found his girlfriend in bed with someone else the week before. That may have explained his attitude. Or did it? If Dave remembered correctly, Enders had told him he wanted to end the relationship with her anyway. Something else was bothering him. He'd have to wait for the right opportunity to ask him some questions.

Dave couldn't help but think back to the last year. Drugs were involved then too. Was it possible that the events last year were somehow connected to what was happening now? In some ways, it seemed unrelated, but he felt he couldn't ignore anything yet. Wouldn't it be great if he could solve both mysteries? It would mean he could finally move on.

He got up with determination and went to his office. With pen and paper he sat behind his desk and wrote out two lists. The first was a list of the things that had happened a year ago; the second was a list of what was happening now.

When he was finished he looked at what he had written. The common thread was drugs. He walked back to his kitchen with the paper in hand. He was disappointed that nothing else had jumped out at him, but that didn't stop him from deciding that these two incidents were related. His every instinct told him that they were. He decided to go back and talk to Jessie. His hand was on the doorknob when there was a knock.

CHAPTER THIRTY-EIGHT

"DON'T LOOK SO surprised, stranger!"

Dave realized his mouth was open; he quickly closed it. "Hello, Claire. Did we have an appointment?"

"No, Dave. I was in the neighborhood so I thought I'd stop by. Aren't you going to invite me in?"

"Oh, sorry, yeah, come on in." He stepped aside to let her enter. As she walked by he could smell her perfume. It had a subtle, sweet smell. It tickled his nose and he had to fight back a sneeze. He closed the door behind her.

"Nice place you have here. Who decorated it?" Claire wandered around the living room. She picked up, looked at, then set down a few pictures and studied the few pieces of bric-a-brac scattered about the room.

"My wife, Beth." He stood by the door, watching her.

"Oh, yes. Well, I guess she did the best she could with what she had." Claire looked at him through lowered lashes. "You'll have to come to my place soon. I had someone decorate it for me. From the city, of course."

"Are you on your way somewhere, Claire?" Dave was annoyed at her insinuation that Beth was a poor decorator; he had always loved how she decorated their home.

"Actually, I'm here to take you out to dinner. I thought we could spend some time together." She sat down on the edge of the couch, careful not to wrinkle her silk suit. She folded her hands in her lap and looked up at him.

"That's nice, Claire, but I'm kind of busy. Maybe if you'd called . . ."

"I tried to call last night and again earlier today. There was no answer." Her mouth drooped in a pout. "Where were you?"

"I was with a friend." He finally moved away from the door and entered the living room. "Would you like a drink?" he offered, hoping he could get rid of her soon.

"That would be nice. White wine, if you have it."

Dave went to the kitchen and returned with two glasses of wine; he handed her one.

Claire took a small sip and then grimaced slightly. She started to say something, and then changed her mind.

"There sure has been a lot of excitement around here these last few days, don't you think? Our small town isn't used to all this. Do you have any idea what's going on, Dave?"

"I'm sure I don't," he replied.

"Oh, Dave, you're straining my neck standing there like that," she patted the spot beside her on the couch. "Come sit beside me."

He walked over and sat on the opposite end of the couch.

"I have no idea what's going on Claire." He sat back and rested one leg on top of the other.

Claire slid over beside him and put her hand on his leg. Dave looked at her. "What are you doing?" he asked.

"I'm a woman who goes after what she wants, Dave, and I've had enough of playing coy with you. I like you a lot. It's been more than a year since your wife died, and you need some female companionship." She moved even closer, so that their thighs were touching, and then she leaned over so her face was hovering close to his, her invitation clear.

Dave was speechless; he'd had no idea she felt this way. He was powerless to resist when she kissed him full on the lips.

Afterward, she sat back to gauge his reaction. He set his wineglass on the coffee table and reached for hers only to find that she had already set hers down. She gazed up at him with passion-filled eyes. He twisted his body around to face her head-on, and then, his hands on her upper arms, he pulled them both to a standing position.

"I'm flattered, Claire, I really am, but I'm just not interested." Then he released her and moved to the other side of the room. He hadn't meant to be so blunt about it.

"What?" she asked, her voice deadly quiet.

"I'm not interested, I'm sorry. You are my accountant, Claire, and a damn good one, but I keep my business and my personal life separate."

"Well, then," she smiled, "I quit as your accountant. There, problem solved."

"No, Claire, I won't let you do that."

"Oh, but I want to," she said as she glided over to stand before him. She put her arms around his neck. "I want you, Dave. I'm not ashamed to admit it. You want me too, admit it."

He realized subtlety wasn't working.

"No, Claire, I don't want you, not that way." He removed her arms and placed them gently by her side. "Now please, I have somewhere I need to be."

Right there before his eyes she changed from a shy seductress into an angry alley cat.

"You bastard!" she spat at him. "How dare you spurn me? I could have done a lot for you. You'll be sorry, just you wait and see," she yelled as she slammed her way out the door.

CHAPTER THIRTY-NINE

I T WAS FRIDAY evening. Jessie had napped for an hour after Dave left. She had tried to come up with another plan of action but she wasn't very successful, so she went back to bed instead. After half an hour of trying to go to sleep, she got up and turned on a light. The pain from her ribs was throbbing again and her muscles were stiff and sore. She walked around the room with slow, measured steps. After a few minutes, her muscles started to loosen up.

In the bathroom, she looked at her reflection in the mirror and grimaced. There were dark circles around her eyes and they looked swollen, as if she hadn't slept for two days. She touched the skin on her cheeks and around her eyes. Then she brushed the abrasion on her forehead, wincing when she got to a tender spot.

She turned the hot water on in the bathtub. While she waited for the tub to fill, she took her clothes off and examined the rest of her body in the mirror. Her side was dark purple with bruises, and when she turned, she noticed a few bruises on her back and shoulders.

As soon as the tub was full enough, she turned the taps off and added some of her favorite bath oil. She lowered herself slowly into the tub, wincing at the sting of the hot water on her bruises. When she was mostly submerged, she lay back and relaxed, letting the heat from the water ease away the ache in her muscles.

She stayed there for a long time, but too soon, the water had cooled to the point where she couldn't enjoy it any longer. She used her toes to pull the plug, and as the water was draining, she slowly pulled herself upright. By the time she could stand up, the bathtub was empty. She closed the shower curtain and turned on the shower to rinse the oil off her body, careful to keep her head bandage dry. The stinging spray felt good on her skin.

She had just managed to pull on her bathrobe when there was a knock on her door. "Just a minute," she yelled out.

She was almost at the door when she thought to ask who was there.

"It's me, Dave."

Jessie opened the door and waved him in. He took in her bathrobe and asked if this was a bad time.

"No, not at all," she told him. "In fact, you're just in time. I want to wash my hair but I can't do it by myself. Would you help me?"

"Sure," he answered, uncertainty visible on his face. "But aren't you still mad at me?"

"We'll get to that, but right now I need you to wash my hair for me. We can do it in the sink." She waved her hand toward the kitchenette sink then went into the bathroom to get what she needed. "Okay, I'm ready."

"It's been a long time since I washed someone's hair for them and then it was my daughter." The sadness was evident on his face only for a moment.

"Give me a moment to get bent over since my muscles are still a bit sore." She took her time, trying to find a comfortable position. She finally settled on a combination of bending and leaning against the counter. "Okay, this should work."

Dave ran the water until he had the right temperature. Taking care to keep her head bandage dry, he washed and conditioned her hair, luxuriating in the feel of it. In no time at all, he was finished and had wrapped a towel around her head.

Jessie walked to the bathroom to towel-dry her hair as much as she could. When she came out it was falling in a tangled mess around her shoulders. She sat down at the small table and began to brush it out.

"Dave . . ."

"Jessie . . ."

They laughed at their timing.

Dave held up his hand. "Jessie, let me go first. I had a lot to think about and I'd like to apologize for slamming out of here the way I did." He had been leaning against the counter by the sink, but now he moved to sit across from Jessie.

"It's okay, Dave." She avoided looking at him by concentrating on her hair.

"No, it's not," he insisted. "I needed to think about things. Something was bothering me but I couldn't put my finger on it. Then I realized that I was thinking about my wife and daughter. I'd like to tell you about it now."

Jessie looked at him now, empathy visible in her gaze. She reached over and put her hand on his. "It's okay, Dave; you don't have to tell me."

"Yes, I do, because it made me realize that I was treating you the same way I was treated. No one believed me and now I doubted you. No, not you exactly, but more the way you're defending your brother. I'm still not convinced that he's not more involved than you want to believe, but . . . anyway, here goes." He got up and walked over to the window, gathering his thoughts while staring unseeing out the window.

"The police came to me and told me they were suspicious about one of my guests. They asked me to help keep an eye on him. You know, keep track of when he went out and when he came back; that sort of thing. I said yes. A few days later, the cops told me they were getting ready to arrest this man. I was to keep the rooms empty on either side of him, so I did. One night they came and arrested him. I figured that was the end of it.

"Then the so-called accident happened." Dave paused while he relived that night again, as he had so many times in his dreams. He took a deep, ragged breath.

"I was devastated. It wasn't until after their funeral that I started to wake up from the void I was in. I just had to understand what had happened out there. I took a drive to the accident scene. Nothing made any sense. I drove up the road looking for something, anything that would explain what had happened. There were tire marks that started a couple of miles before, before where they went off the road. It didn't make sense! If Beth was driving too fast to make the corner, why were there skid marks two miles before the turn?

"I parked the car and walked along the highway, trying to piece things together. Then it hit me. Someone had tried to run her off the road. If she was going too fast for the corner it was because she was trying to get away from something or someone.

"I went to Jones with what I thought had happened but he didn't believe me. At least I don't think he did. He said the marks were inconclusive. Without a witness, there was no way to prove what had happened." He turned to face Jessie, his eyes wet with tears.

"So you see, I can't just say that the cops have the right person. I may not be convinced that they don't but you are. I want to help you find out the truth, whatever that is."

Jessie slowly got up from the table and moved over to where he stood. She placed her hand gently on his arm and looked up at him.

"Dave, thanks for telling me. I can't imagine the horror and pain you must have gone through and are still going through. I wonder, though, could any of that have anything to do with what's happening now?" She shook her head in answer to her own question. "No, that seems too farfetched."

"Thanks, Jessie," he smiled.

"For what?"

"That's what I had started thinking, that maybe events are related somehow." He pulled the piece of paper from his shirt pocket. "I wrote down what I know about the two incidents. The only thing they have in common though, as far as I can see, is that there are drugs involved." He handed the paper to her. "Here, take a look and tell me what you think."

She accepted the paper and turned to the light to study it.

"I see what you mean," she said finally. "There's got to be something we're missing." She walked over and sat down at the table.

"Wait," she said a few minutes later. "There has to be a way to get more information. From what Brant told me, this guy, Dickie, may be able to tell us what we need to know. We need to find him. If we can get him alone, maybe we can convince him to talk to us. It's worth a shot." She looked over at him. "What do you think?"

Dave thought about it, trying to work it through in his mind.

"Well, we know that this Stack guy isn't going to talk to us. The only other person – as far as we know – who would know what Stack is up to would be Dickie." He nodded to himself. "I say we give it a try, but not tonight."

"I want to argue, but my better sense is agreeing with you, Dave. I know I need some more sleep and hopefully I won't be quite so sore tomorrow." She walked over to him and looked deep into his eyes. "Thank you, Dave, for sticking with me in this." Before she could chicken out, she stood on her tiptoes and kissed him gently on the side of his mouth, ignoring the protesting pull from her muscles.

He cupped her face in his hands and leaned over so she could stand flat on her feet and then he kissed her back, fully on the mouth. When he was finished, they both had to catch their breath.

"Wow," Jessie whispered. She took his hand and led him over to the bed. She pulled him down to sit beside her. "Dave . . ." she hesitated.

"What is it, Jessie?" he asked, concern filled his voice.

"Dave, I really like you," she finally said, blushing.

"Jessie, I really like you too." He used his left index finger to lift her face toward his. "But . . . ?"

"Stop me if I'm wrong, but this feels like we're about to do something." She was having a hard time looking him straight in the eyes, but his gentle pressure was stopping her from lowering her face and her gaze.

"Yes, I feel that too. It's okay if you don't want it to go any further, Jessie." He locked his gaze with hers, forcing her to see that he was telling her the truth.

"I do want it, I think. That's just it, Dave. I'm so confused right now. My main concern is for Brant, but I feel such a strong pull toward you. It scares me." She put her left arm around his back and laid her head on his shoulders.

"It's okay, Jessie." He hugged her gently. "I'm confused too. So maybe, until we know for sure what we want, we could just be there for each other. How does that sound?" He brushed her hair away from her face, enjoying the physical contact.

"Oh, Dave, that sounds great," she replied, the relief obvious in her voice.

He gave her shoulders a quick squeeze, and then he got up and went to the door. He flashed a quick smile, and then he was gone.

CHAPTER FORTY

THE SUN SHINING in the window woke her up the next morning. She lay there for a few minutes thinking about the night before. She smiled to herself as she remembered how Dave had said that he liked her a lot too.

She sat up slowly; her muscles were still sore but the pain was a little better and her headache was only a dull thud.

In the bathroom, she piled her hair on top of her head so she could work her shower cap on. The hot water cascading down her back felt like a massage, it was so soothing. She extended her muscles until the pain was too much and then did it again. Before too long she had most of her flexibility back.

She was dressed and taking her medication when there was a knock on her door.

"Dave!" she exclaimed when she opened the door to see him standing there with a breakfast tray in his hands.

"I stopped by a little while ago but you must have been in the shower. I figured it would be safe enough to cook us some breakfast. Are you hungry?" As he talked, he set the food on the table.

With a smile on her face, she sat down and they ate, chatting about anything but what they had planned for the day.

Jessie was sitting on the patio steps when Dave came back from taking their dirty dishes away. He handed her some fresh coffee and then sat beside her.

"Okay, Dave, what's the plan?"

"I thought we'd go by Domer's place. We can sit and watch for this Dickie guy to leave and then talk to him. What do you think?"

"It sounds like a plan to me," she agreed, nodding.

In Dave's truck, they pulled over a few houses down from Domer's. Dave shut the truck off and they waited. It was early Saturday afternoon and everything looked quiet. There were a few people out and about, cutting lawns and gardening. Once in a while a car would drive by.

Before long, their attention began to wander. It was difficult to just sit there and do nothing. Jessie studied the neighborhood. Most of the houses were in some state of disrepair. A few were kept up; meaning the yards were clean and free of junk.

"Here we go," Dave said.

Jessie looked around. Someone had just left the house and was walking down the street, away from them.

"That's him!" she said, tapping Dave on the arm, excited. "What do we do now?"

"Let's just follow him for a while and see where he goes. Hopefully an opportunity will present itself." He started the truck and pulled out on the street. He kept his speed down and stayed back far enough so that Dickie wouldn't spot them. He didn't need to worry; Dickie didn't pay any attention to his surroundings.

"It looks like he's going to cut down that alley," Dave said. "We'll catch him from the other side." He sped up and went around the block and then entered the alley. They could see Dickie ahead of them.

Dickie looked up when he heard the truck and moved to the side of the alley to allow them room to pass. When the vehicle stopped in front of him, he shrugged and stopped as well.

Dave was the first one out of the truck. "Are you Dickie?" he asked.

"I might be," Dickie replied, suspicious. "Who are you?"

Dave looked back toward the truck at Jessie. She climbed out. "Remember me?" she asked him.

"No." He looked at her and thought for a minute. "Oh, yeah, right, you're Lane's sister, right?"

"Yes, that's me. I want you to answer a few questions for me," she said as she walked up to him.

"Really? What makes you think I'll tell you anything?" he glared at her.

"Because I say so," Dave answered him.

"And just who the hell are you?"

"I'm a friend. Now answer the lady's questions."

Dickie looked from Dave to Jessie and back again. "Just what do you think I have to say to the two of you?"

"I want to know why you and Stack are still here," Jessie told him.

"I don't know nothin'," was the reply.

Dave rushed at Dickie and pushed him up against a fence. He held him there and glared into his eyes. "Answer the lady's question," he snarled.

Dickie was startled, and that wasn't something that normally happened to him. He looked into the other man's eyes and didn't like what he saw. He would have to say something but his mind wasn't working fast enough to come up with anything, except maybe the possibility of making some quick cash. These two looked pretty desperate. "What's it worth to ya?"

Dave narrowed his eyes and moved his face within inches of Dickie's. "Are you trying to shake us down?" he growled. "Oh please, say it isn't so."

Now Dickie was nervous. His eyes locked with Dave's, he felt like a cornered rat so he did the only thing he knew to do, he lashed out. The blow caught Dave on the shoulder and glanced off.

"What was that?" he asked. "Are you some kind of momma's boy? Do you really want to do this the hard way?"

Dickie didn't even see it coming although he should have expected it. The punch landed in his soft stomach, which caused the air to whoosh out of his lungs. He doubled over in pain, his breaths coming in short, fast gasps. He lifted his head slightly and looked at Dave. Dave hit him again, this time an upper cut, which flung Dickie's head back and knocked him to the ground with a thump.

Dave stood over him and looked down at him with disgust. He looked around for Jessie and finally saw her backed up on the other side of the truck with her hand on her mouth. He rushed over to her.

"Are you okay?" he asked her.

She nodded. "Was all that really necessary?"

"Oh, yes, it was," he answered as he rubbed his sore knuckles. "Let's go see if he's ready to talk now."

They walked over to Dickie who still lay on the ground. Dave bent over and grabbed him by the shirt and hauled him to his feet.

"Are you ready to answer her questions now?"

Dickie wiped the blood from his split lip as he kept a wary eye on Dave. "Yeah, sure."

"Well?" Dave prodded, "why are you guys still here?"

"I could get myself killed for telling you this," Dickie responded, the fear easy to read in his eyes.

"Do you need some more persuading?" Dave lifted a clenched fist.

"No, no, that's okay," Dickie held up his hands in surrender. He wiped his mouth again, stalling for time. "Stack has been meeting with someone, I don't know who. I think he's trying to get his drugs back."

"Who has he been meeting with?" Jessie asked.

"I don't know I said." He held his hands up again. "No, really, I don't know who they are. Stack's been meeting with a couple of people, making plans of some kind. He won't tell me anything, just said to wait until I was called on. He's gone out for the day, says he'll be back later and to be ready to move." He snuck a quick look at them to see if they were buying it.

"What about Brant? What's his involvement?"

"He's just a stupid kid," Dickie spit with disgust. "Doesn't know his ass from a hole in the ground."

"Who killed John Domer?"

"I don't know. Your brother's in jail for it, maybe he did it." He looked at Jessie with a sneer on his face.

"Don't sass the lady." Dave moved toward him as if to hit him again.

Dickie backed away. "Look," he said, "I told you all I know. If you want more information you'll have to talk to Stack." Good luck, he thought.

Dave looked at Jessie. "What do you think? Is there anything else you want to ask him?"

"I think this," she gestured toward Dickie, "this jerk knows more than he's saying but it seems the man with all the answers is Stack. Why would he tell this," she pointed at Dickie again, "any more than he had to? Obviously he's a weak link. Let's try to set up a meeting with Stack."

Dickie watched them drive away, a small self-satisfied smile on his face; they'd bought it hook, line and sinker.

CHAPTER FORTY-ONE

"**I** DON'T LIKE THIS, Jessie," Dave said as he slowly got out of the truck. He reached behind the seat and pulled out the tire iron he kept there.

They were parked in front of an abandoned warehouse. At one time it had been a sorting plant for the area's farmers. They would harvest their potatoes and carrots and bring them here for cleaning and sorting. They would then be stored in the cool rooms until they were shipped off to market. A few years earlier, the warehouse had been left empty when the owner had gone bankrupt.

Jessie got out of the truck and walked over to him.

"I know what you mean," she said. "This place feels kind of, I don't know, dead."

"I still can't believe you got Stack to agree to meet us."

"I'm not sure how I did it," she said, thinking over the conversation. They had gone back to the motel after their encounter with Dickie. Jessie had decided to try the direct approach and called Domer's place, hoping that Stack would be there but not expecting it, according to what Dickie had told them. She was surprised when he answered the phone.

"This is Jessie Lane," she had said. "We need to talk."

"We sure do. Meet me at the old Philton place, tomorrow at noon. Your boyfriend will know where it is."

Jessie had hung up the phone thinking that had been too easy. She had repeated the conversation to Dave on their way to dinner.

Now, standing in front of the abandoned building, her doubts came flooding back.

"I'm not sure about this now, either," she said, putting her hand on his arm. "This meeting was way too easy to arrange. I didn't really tell you but Stack didn't argue at all about meeting with us. It's almost as if he wanted to meet with us but that doesn't make any sense."

"Now you tell me," he said, shaking his head. "Well, we're here now so we might as well see what's up. Stay close behind me," he ordered her.

They made their way down the side of the building, on the lookout for a door. They found one three-quarters of the way down. Dave stopped and looked around, not too sure what he was looking for but checking just the same. He reached out and grabbed the doorknob. It was stiff, but it opened without too much effort. As he swung the door inward, the hinges groaned in protest. Jessie jumped at the sound and grabbed onto Dave's arm.

"I don't like this," she whispered.

Dave motioned for her to keep quiet. They stepped inside the door and stood still for a few moments while their eyes adjusted to the gloom.

They were at the edge of a large room. Against the far wall, they could just make out some kind of machine with a long conveyor belt attached to it. To the left were huge sliding doors, obviously used for trucks to drive in and out. To their right was an office and a long hallway, possibly leading to the cold storage rooms.

Dave inched his way forward slowly, wishing he'd brought a flashlight. His grip tightened on the tire iron; it was too quiet.

As if she read his mind, Jessie chose that moment to yell at the top of her lungs: "Hello!" Her voice echoed in the cavernous room.

"Shit!" Dave whirled around. "You scared me half to death! What the hell did you do that for?"

"I was tired of feeling scared," she told him. "Stack is supposed to be here, and we're not expecting anything weird. Besides, I just needed to release some tension."

"Well, next time give me some warning, would you?"

"Sorry. Let's go and check around over here first," she suggested.

They walked over to the far wall where the huge machine sat. By now their eyes were adjusted to the gloom and they were able to see everywhere except the deepest shadowy areas. They didn't find anything interesting so they headed for the office.

Inside the small room there was an old desk, a filing cabinet with its drawers hanging open and a couple of old, rickety chairs.

"I don't see anything of interest," said Dave. "Let's head to the back, to the storage area."

Jessie stepped around him to go behind the desk and a scream tore from her mouth, echoing in the room.

"What is it?" he asked as he rushed over to her.

She couldn't speak so she just pointed down at the floor. Dave grabbed her shoulders and looked down where she indicated.

There lay a body, obviously dead, possibly Stack. Just to make sure he was dead, Dave moved Jessie out of the way and knelt down to check for a pulse, setting down the tire iron. He wasn't able to find one.

"He is definitely dead," he said unnecessarily. "I'm going to assume this is Stack. He hasn't been dead for very long though, he's still warm. It looks like someone wanted to make sure the job was done."

The body lay on its side with the head thrown back. It was hard to see but Dave could make out at least two gunshot wounds, one to the chest and one to the head. As he was looking around he thought he saw something else.

"What?" he asked no one in particular. He leaned over the body and pulled on the object. It was heavy and slick with blood. With one hand on top of the desk, he leaned under and felt around for something that he could grab. He finally felt a handle. With a heave, he pulled out a large satchel. It was latched shut so he worked at it to get it open, a gasp escaping him at the contents.

"Oh my god," was all he could say. Inside the satchel were bundles of cash and bags of white powder, most likely cocaine. He let the bag drop.

"Let's get the hell out of here," he said as he grabbed Jessie's arm and pulled her from the room. He ran with her out of the warehouse and in to the bright, noon sunshine.

Jessie immediately doubled over, throwing up over and over until there was nothing left. She slowly straightened up, grimacing with the pain in her ribs. "Ohmygod, ohmygod," she kept saying.

Dave walked over to her and put his arms around her. "It's okay, Jessie, let's get out of here. We'll go to the police." They would have to be told about *everything* they had found. He slowly led her toward his truck.

"Hold it right there."

They stopped and slowly turned. Dave's eyes opened wide with shock; Jessie gasped in fear.

CHAPTER FORTY-TWO

S HE WAS STANDING four meters away from them, her legs shoulder width apart with a 9mm Beretta gripped firmly in her hands and pointed at them.

"Claire?"

Dave started toward her.

"Stop right there, Dave," she snarled. "Don't come any closer."

"What's this all about, Claire?"

"Never mind that right now," She waved the gun at them, motioned them to walk around her. "Move it."

Dave kept his arm tight around Jessie's shoulders. He had to force her to move, she was so stiff from shock. They moved past Claire and went back the way they had just come.

"Where are we going?" he asked.

"Just never mind. Follow my orders and you may live to see tomorrow. Maybe." She laughed, the evil sound sending shivers up his back.

They walked along the building. Dave hesitated once but Claire jabbed him in the back with the gun. She meant business.

They rounded the end of the building and saw a dark blue Jimmy parked there. Claire motioned for them to get in the front while she climbed in back, her gun aimed at the back of Dave's head. She handed him the keys and told him to start it.

"Drive around the warehouse," she ordered. "When you get to the road, turn right."

Half an hour later they pulled on to a dirt track. It was very bumpy and tossed them around on their seats.

Except for directions from their captor, not a word was spoken.

Jessie was gripping the armrest on the door, her knuckles white with the strain. Dave kept both hands on the steering wheel; the only visible sign of tension was his clenching jaw.

The jarring served to bring Jessie out of her catatonic state. The pain she felt at each jolt increased her awareness. She wanted to speak but the tension inside the vehicle stopped her.

Up ahead was a log cabin. Dave stopped the vehicle in front of it and turned off the motor.

Claire was the first one out of the vehicle. She opened Jessie's door and motioned her out with the gun. As soon as her feet touched the ground, Claire grabbed her around the neck and held the gun to her head.

"Okay Dave, now it's your turn. Get out slowly and keep both hands where I can see them. If you try anything funny, I'll shoot her right now. Got it?"

He nodded and slowly eased out of the Jimmy.

"Go inside the cabin," she ordered. "The door is unlocked."

If this had been any other time, Dave may have liked what he saw. The only thing 'cabin' about the place was its location. There were wide steps leading up to a large patio, where a few Adirondack chairs sat overlooking the hills.

He opened the door and stepped inside. The first things he saw were two chairs, one on each side of the large room, with large pieces of rope hanging off them. Between the chairs sat a couch and a coffee table.

"Okay, you," Claire said, shove Jessie into the room. "Tie Dave to this chair," she pointed to the nearest one. "Use the ropes that are already there. Dave, get in the chair or I swear to God I'll shoot her."

Dave sat in the chair that she indicated. Jessie proceeded to secure the ropes.

"Make sure they're nice and tight, we don't want Dave getting any dumb ideas."

Dave spoke for the first time since they had left the warehouse. "What's going on Claire? Why are you doing this?" He looked at her closely. There was a maniacal glint in her eyes.

"Oh, gee, should I tell you? Well, why not? First, though, I'll check these ropes, you know, make sure they're nice and tight. You. Bitch." She pointed at Jessie. "Go and sit in the other chair." She bent down and tugged on the ropes. Satisfied, she straightened up and then headed for Jessie's chair.

Dave looked at Jessie and saw that her eyes had glazed with shock again. He tried and finally caught her gaze and sent her a comforting glance. She responded by shaking her head a little and trying to smile.

"You know this is all your fault," Claire told Jessie. "If you hadn't shown up here none of this would've happened."

"What do you mean?" Jessie managed to croak out. "Ouch!"

Claire was tightening the rope around Jessie's left leg; her movements were jerky and angry. She had put the gun on the floor beside her. Jessie made a sideways move for it; the chair came crashing down which knocked Claire over. Jessie scrambled for the gun but Claire beat her to it.

"That was stupid," she said as she backhanded Jessie across the face. "Now get that chair upright and sit in it! No more of your crap or I'll shoot you!"

Jessie got back in the chair and held her hand to her cheek.

"If you hadn't come here Dave would be mine," Claire yelled at her, finishing her task. "But no, you had to show up and be the poor little bitch in trouble."

"What are you talking about, Claire?" Dave asked. His heartbeat was slowly getting back to normal after Jessie's grab for the gun. "What makes you think I would be yours?"

"You really don't know? I was the one that got rid of your stupid wife and bratty kid," she bragged to him. "They didn't deserve you! I did. And if it wasn't for her," she slapped Jessie again, "you would have turned to me already."

Dave felt the blood drain from his face. Claire killed his wife and daughter? Because of some sick, twisted love thing? He shook his head to clear it.

Jessie had felt tears spring to her eyes when Claire had slapped her and now they welled up again. She blinked rapidly to clear them, her concern now was for Dave. She saw the shock and despair on his face.

"I don't believe it. Why would you kill them? They didn't do anything to you!" He could feel the anger building, growing like a rapid cancer in his belly.

Claire gave one last yank to Jessie's ropes and then she walked over to Dave.

"I hadn't planned on it at first," she told him. "But then you helped the cops bust a friend of mine. I lost a lot of money because of you! You had to pay."

"Why? Why did you do it?"

Claire stood in front of Dave. She reached out and placed her hand on his cheek. Her eye softened for a brief moment. "Because you and I are meant for each other. I knew it the first time I saw you. Do you remember?" Her eyes took on a dreamy look as she remembered. "You 'accidentally' bumped into me in the grocery store. Remember?"

He shook his head no.

Claire let her hand fall to her side. Her eyes became cold with that slightly crazed look again.

"Of course you remember. Think about it! I followed you that day. You were new in town, and when I saw you with your wife and daughter I thought all was lost. Then you asked me to be your accountant. I couldn't believe it! All that time we spent together, it made me want you even more. I didn't know how I was going to accomplish it, our being together. Then you helped the cops. You betrayed me!"

Like a lightning flash she slapped him, so hard his head was flung back. An angry red welt surfaced on his cheek. Claire walked away and then turned back.

"My drug connection was here to bring me a new shipment. I had a feeling something was wrong, so I made him wait a few days. I was right. I let him think the buy would go down that night, the night he was arrested. The cops got the dope, and I was left with nothing. Thank God I hadn't paid for it yet. That really would have been tragic!" She shook her head as she remembered.

"I had to go to the city to get what I needed, but first I had to lay low for a few days to make sure I wasn't suspected. I knew you had fingered him because I had been watching you and I saw you talking to Jones. I was on my way back when I spotted your station wagon ahead of me. I could see that you weren't in it, so I seized the moment. Do you want me to tell you how it happened? How frightened they were?"

Dave's mind was screaming, "No!" No, he didn't want to hear, but he could feel his head moving slowly up and down.

"No!" Jessie screamed for him. "Haven't you done enough already?" She was straining against the ropes that held her.

"You, shut up!" Claire yelled back at her. "Beth was frantic," she told Dave. "She kept looking in the rearview mirror. Every time I hit the car I could tell that she screamed. The little girl I couldn't see, but I know she was scared. Then we were getting closer and closer to the turn. I knew it was now or never. I gunned the engine and the car was going off the road! I stopped as fast as I could on the side of the road and got out just in time to see the explosion." She laughed. "It was so easy! I got back in my car and went home. No one ever suspected a thing," she smiled to herself.

Jessie was horrified. She looked over at Dave. His head was hung low and she could see the tears rolling off his face, soaking his shirtfront.

"You are one sick, twisted human being!" she yelled at Claire. "Dave, are you okay? Dave?"

Claire was so lost in her world of memories that she did not hear Jessie at all.

Dave slowly lifted his head; his eyes were filled with the pain of what he had just heard. He had been right, he'd known it all along but to hear it confirmed in such detail was excruciating. It was like they were dead all over again. He focused on Jessie, trying to regain some composure. If he fell apart now it would be the end for them, literally.

Jessie watched as he struggled with himself. Slowly his eyes cleared, and the tears were replaced with steel determination. Jessie tried to send him looks of support and he smiled his thanks.

"You are not," he cleared his throat, "going to get away with this." His voice got stronger with every syllable.

Claire turned to him, snapped out of her reverie. "Says who? You're not going anywhere."

The sound of a vehicle caught her attention. She moved over to the window and looked outside.

CHAPTER FORTY-THREE

CLAIRE WATCHED AS the car stopped behind the Jimmy then she opened the door and walked outside.

"Dave, are you okay?" Jessie whispered.

"No, I'm not," he whispered back. "But I will be. Can you see who's here?"

Jessie tried to swing around to look but she couldn't see very far outside. "No," she said, "my angle is all wrong." She looked worriedly at Dave. "I know what she said was hard for you to hear. Try not to think about it, at least until we can think of a way out of here."

"Oh, I'm way ahead of you on that," he said, determination strong in his voice. "If anything, what she's told us so far is adding to my resolve to somehow get us out of this mess. Are you okay?"

"I'm sore as hell, but I'll live, I think." She smiled weakly at him.

They stopped talking as they heard voices approaching as Claire and her companion came in the cabin.

"Dickie!" Jessie exclaimed. "What are you doing here?"

"Aw shit, Claire. I thought you said you had taken care of everything." He stopped just inside the room.

Claire grabbed his arm and pulled him the rest of the way inside. "I was just telling them how they ruined my life when you got here." She slammed the door shut.

"What have you told them about us?"

"Nothing. Yet."

"Damn it, Claire, I thought we had a deal!"

"We do, now shut up." Claire turned to Jessie. "I hope you're happy. All that has happened in the last few days is because of you."

"What do you mean?"

"Stack was an old enemy of mine. Back in the early days of my drug career, he almost got me killed. When he showed up here looking for his drugs, I ran into him. He had forgotten all about me! At first I was mad but then I soon got over it, especially when he started flirting with me. Men!

"In order to find my opportunity for revenge, I played along, made like I was interested in him. As soon as he realized he wouldn't get his dope back he turned to my business and me. He found out where I hid my stash and threatened to steal it from me unless I paid him. Fat chance of that!

"I met your brother and convinced him that I could help him out of his dilemma. What a patsy! I got him to snoop for me and a few days ago, he told me Stack was bragging about all the money he was making from this trip, how lucky your brother was that something better had come along. He was talking about my stuff! I couldn't let him get away with that.

"I had to get your brother out of the way. I told him Domer was after you and I made sure he could get away to follow Domer. Your brother didn't kill Domer, I did! It served him right because he was ripping me off too!" Claire's eyes lit up at the memory.

"You?" Jessie gasped.

"Yes, me." She grabbed Dickie's arm. "Let's go."

They headed for the back of the cabin. Dave and Jessie tried to listen in on their conversation but they were too far away.

"I don't like the look of this," Dave said.

"I think you're right," Jessie agreed. "We have to do something. She must have killed Stack. She's crazy, Dave. Can you move at all?"

"Yes, she killed him all right, but I don't think she noticed that her drugs and money were there. I saw them under the desk where we found Stack, in a black satchel." He was trying to move his arms but the ropes were too tight and only allowed a slight movement. "I can hardly move, how about you?"

"About the same. Did you say Stack had her drugs and cash? I wonder if she knows? What are we going to do?" Jessie had been fighting to keep control but she was losing the battle. Claire was a monster!

"Take it easy," Dave tried to soothe her as he noticed her panicked state. "I'll think of something." He kept trying to move his arms and legs. He felt the chair start to creak with his efforts. Keeping watch toward the back of the cabin for Claire and Dickie, he worked at loosening the back slats of the chair. The sound of the two of them arguing helped to cover up the sounds of the breaking chair. They were able to make out the odd word here and there from the back.

" . . . dead!"

"I . . . alone!"

"Are they saying what I think they're saying? Dave?" Jessie was trying to look in all directions; her head was moving around so fast she looked like her neck was a slinky. "She's planning to murder us, isn't she?"

Dave had started the chair rocking, his face red with the effort.

"I'm . . . trying . . . to . . . get . . . loose."

All at once he fell over. One side of the chair back cracked under his weight. He stayed still long enough to make sure they hadn't heard him; then with some effort, he managed to get onto his side. He worked at the chair until the weak side broke away.

Now that he could move one arm it was easier to break the other side. Quickly, he worked at untying his hands As soon as that was done, he untied his legs. He was about to untie Jessie when they heard Claire coming back to the living room. He scrambled to find a hiding place. This part of the cabin was fairly wide open with no easy place to conceal someone. He spied a set of stairs leading to the loft; the space below the stair was used for storage. He managed to worm his way in between old coats and some boxes that were piled there.

Just as he slid from view, Claire walked into the room.

"Where is he?" she screamed at Jessie.

Jessie shrugged in response.

Claire kicked at the chair and rope fragments, and then ran about the room. She looked under the couch, outside the door and in the fireplace; she found nothing. She ran over to stand in front of Jessie.

"Where the hell is he?" she demanded.

"I don't know," Jessie answered defiantly. "Maybe he just disappeared."

Jessie didn't see it coming; Claire used the butt of her gun as club and hit her behind the left ear. Jessie slumped over, unconscious.

"Okay, Dave," Claire crooned, "where are you? I've knocked out your girlfriend; I may have even killed her. Why don't you come and save her?" She checked out a few more possible hiding places; behind the drapes, under the coffee table. Next she headed for the closet.

Dave watched her walk past him. The closet was opposite where he was standing. He forced himself to push back even further into the stairwell. His elbow bumped against something but he managed to catch it before it fell to the floor.

Claire stood beside the closet door and pointed the gun with one hand while she reached out for the door handle with the other one. She pulled it open quickly and swept it with the gun but it was empty. Back beside the broken chair she started talking again.

"You are so dead, mister. I gave you every chance to be with me, but no; you'd rather be with this bitch. Maybe I should just shoot her now and save us the trouble later on." She walked over to where Jessie sat, still unconscious.

"Dickie! Get in here now!"

CHAPTER FORTY-FOUR

DICKIE CAME TROTTING out, his body shaking with the effort, his breathing hard and fast.

Claire pointed the gun at him.

Dickie stopped where he was, just inside the room. "What are doing, pointing that thing at me?" he asked. "What happened in here?"

"Dave got free. I can't find him. He's in here somewhere."

"You stupid bitch! I told you, you should have killed them back at the warehouse." Dickie started toward Claire, intent on taking the gun away from her.

Claire took a step back, coolly aimed and then fired.

Dickie was mid-stride and teetered there for a second before he fell over. The shot to the head had killed him instantly.

"There now, isn't that better?" Claire giggled like a little schoolgirl. "Claire doesn't like to be called a stupid bitch." Abruptly, the giggle was replaced with a twisted grin. "Now, Dave, I've had just about enough of this. Come out like a good little boy. I'll shoot Jessie and then we can be together. As soon as I find where Stack hid my money we can go far, far away, where no one will know us. I'll have your babies and you'll forget all about your old family. What do you say?"

She walked over to the couch and patted the seat beside her. "Come on, Dave. Come and sit beside me." Then her voice changed from coaxing to cold. "Come here or I'll shoot her."

She waited for one minute.

"No? You don't want to sit with me? Fine." She got up and walked over to Jessie.

Jessie was just starting to come around. She was still a bit groggy and watched Claire through uncomprehending eyes.

Claire stood in front of Jessie and raised the gun until it rested against Jessie's forehead.

"Say good-bye, lover boy."

CHAPTER FORTY-FIVE

"NOOOO!"

Dave had been slowly extricating himself from his hiding place. He had just rounded the stairwell when Claire walked over to Jessie. He rushed at her and reached her before she could swing the gun on him. From two meters away he launched himself at her. The force of his tackle sent them both flying and they ended up in a tangle on the floor.

Jessie looked on in horror, now fully alert. She felt helpless and strained at the bonds that held her in place. She ignored the sharp stabs of pain that sliced across her middle.

Claire and Dave struggled, rolling over and over on the floor, both of them full of rage. Claire had managed to maintain hold of the gun and she was trying to shoot in Jessie's direction but she was struggling to keep any kind of aim. Dave tried to take the gun but Claire's madness had given her an added strength.

He finally managed to gain a hold on her gun hand. He struggled to take the gun away from her or to at least keep it pointed away from Jessie.

Jessie watched the gun appear and disappear. She tried to scream but nothing would come out. They were rolling around so much that she couldn't keep track of who had control of the gun.

Then, all of a sudden, Claire was on top of Dave and he was holding her gun hand. They were struggling for control when the gun went off.

CHAPTER FORTY-SIX

"DAVE!" JESSIE SCREAMED. "Dave!"

"I'm okay," he managed to grunt.

He pushed Claire off his midsection. She was dying; the shot had gone into her chest, hitting her heart. She was gasping for breath. Dave laid her on the floor and brushed the hair away from her face.

"Oh, Claire, what have you done?" he asked, feeling sorry for her now.

"I . . . I wanted it all," she gasped. "I'm dying, aren't' I?"

"Yes," was all he could say.

"We . . . could've . . . had it . . . all." One last breath and she was gone.

Dave got up and untied Jessie. He picked her up and took her to the couch. They sat there for a long time, just holding each other. Soon enough, the real world intruded and caused Jessie to wince at the old and new pains.

"What do we do now?" she asked.

"We have to call the police. There are going to be a lot of questions and they probably won't let us be together until they're satisfied about our part in all this." He cupped her face in his hands. "I was so scared, Jessie. She would have killed you. She was crazy. I didn't kill her though, the gun just went off."

"I know, Dave." Now it was her turn to comfort him. "It's okay, it'll all be okay." She put her arms around him and hugged him, despite the pain it caused.

"Okay. I'm okay for now." He got up. "I'm going to go look for a phone."

He came back a few minutes later.

"Jessie? Jessie where are you?" He searched everywhere in the room for her, carefully avoiding the two bodies. Then he noticed the front door was open. He went outside and found her sitting in one of the deck chairs, looking out at the hills.

"There you are," he said. "I thought I'd lost you there for a minute. The police are on their way."

Jessie looked up at his with tears in her eyes. "I can't believe all this has happened." She gestured toward the inside of the cabin. "If I hadn't come here, no one would have died. It's all my fault."

"Oh, Jessie, no," he was quick to reassure her. "You didn't kill anyone, you weren't the greedy one." A sob caught in his throat. "You certainly didn't kill my family." He turned away so she wouldn't see his tears.

She pulled herself out of the chair and went to him and put her arms around his waist. They stood like that until the police showed up.

The next few hours were a blur. They were both handcuffed and taken back to town. At the detachment, they were taken to separate rooms to be interviewed. Their stories were too incredible to be believed, especially when they both described events the same way.

Stack's body was recovered from the warehouse along with the cocaine and cash. Initial reports showed that Claire's gun had been used to kill him although further tests would confirm it.

"You are one lucky person," Jones remarked to Jessie.

"I don't feel like it and I have the bruised ribs and headache to prove it," she responded. "What's happening with my brother?"

"He admitted stashing the drugs in your car. He will be charged with possession with intent to traffic. He'll probably get off with probation since this is his first offense. When I asked him why he confessed to possession, he said it was time for him to take some responsibility for his actions."

"Good for him. I hope he's learned his lesson. Where is he now?"

"We're going to keep him here until he goes to court, then we'll arrange transportation back to Ontario."

"Can I see him?" she asked.

Jones thought about it for a minute. "Sure. Sit tight and I'll have him brought in."

She sat and waited patiently. Finally the door opened and Brant walked in.

"Jessie!" He gave her a quick hug. When she gasped in pain he released her and looked at her more closely. "What happened to you? Are you all right?"

They sat down.

"I am now. A lot has happened since the last time I saw you."

"Yeah, I heard about some of it. Tell me."

Jessie told him everything about being beat up, finding Stack dead then being kidnapped and almost murdered.

"Claire confessed to killing John." She turned in her chair to face him. "She also told me she met you, that you were helping her."

"Yeah, I met her," he admitted sheepishly. "She seemed real nice, said she'd help me. What a sucker I was! Jessie, I'm so sorry about all of this. If it wasn't for me, none of this would have happened."

"What's done is done," she said, forgiving him. How could she not? "We have to go on from here. I am proud of you for owning up to your responsibility. It wasn't easy for you, I know."

"Sitting in jail has given me a lot of time to think about things. I called Linda and talked to her for a long time. She's been thinking about a lot of things too. She asked me to ask you to call her, when you feel up to it." He looked her in the eyes. "She's real sorry, Jess. I hope you two can patch things up. I love you both and I want us to be a family again. Will you think about it?"

"I've got a lot of things to sort through, Brant, but I will think about it." She leaned over and hugged him. "I have to go now, but I'll come back and see you tomorrow."

"That's okay, Jessie, you don't have to. But I would like you to be there when I go to court."

"It's a deal." When she stood so did Brant. They hugged again for a few minutes and then walked out of the room together.

Dave was waiting for them.

Brant walked up and shook his hand, introducing himself. "I understand that I have you to thank for keeping Jessie safe. Thank you." An officer led Brant back to his cell.

Dave put his arm around Jessie's shoulders. "Let's go."

CHAPTER FORTY-SEVEN

DAVE PULLED TO a stop in front of the motel. The police had been kind enough to bring his truck back to the detachment. He shut the motor off, and they sat there quietly for a while.

"Jessie . . ."

"Dave . . ."

They laughed.

"Seems like we've done this before." He laughed.

"You go first, Dave."

"Jessie, I," he struggled for the right words. "I'm sorry. About today, I should have insisted we go to the police instead of trying to handle this by ourselves. I'm sorry."

"No, Dave, I'm the one who's sorry." She shook her head. "If I wasn't so pigheaded we wouldn't have been in the mess we were in."

The silence stretched out between them.

"Where do we go from here?" he finally asked.

"I don't know."

She turned slowly toward him. He looked at her.

"I need some time, Dave, and so do you. Claire hit you pretty hard with what she told you, and now you need some time to digest it."

"Yes, I do." He nodded in agreement. "What will you do?"

"I want to spend some time with Aunt Mae. I need to get some answers about a few things, and I think that's the place I need to be to do it."

"Okay, that sounds good. What about us?"

"We've only known each other, what, a week? It's hard to believe it's only been that long. I feel as if I've known you forever."

"Unreal, yes it is." He reached for her hand. "If there's anything here for us, I'd like to explore it. How do you feel?"

Jessie heard alarm bells going off in her head. This was too much, too soon. She pushed her thoughts away. "I feel the same, but I can't deal with it right now," she told him. "Right now all I'd like to do is have a bath and go to bed."

"Okay," he said, turning away. He reached for the door handle. "If that's the way you feel about it."

"Dave, please wait."

He turned back, his eyes questioning.

"I . . ." She felt awkward. "I would really like it if you stayed with me tonight and just held me. I think we could both use some comforting. Don't you?"

He looked at her for so long and so intently that she began to wonder if she had said the wrong thing.

"I'd like that very much, Jessie."

They made their way to Jessie's room; he helped her in and out of the bath and then tucked her into bed. Not a word was exchanged. They both lay in bed just holding each other.

The next morning, Jessie called her aunt. Mae was happy to hear from her and assured her she was still welcome to stay as long as she wanted to.

After she got her car from the impound lot, she drove out to Mae's. On the way there, she went over her parting from Dave. It had been difficult.

"I don't know how long it will be," she had said.

"Take as long as you need to," he had told her. "You know where to find me." Then he had given her a hug and a kiss and waved as she left. He didn't see her tears.

Jessie pulled up to the house where Mae was waiting for her, sitting on the porch. As she climbed out of the car, Mae came down the steps to meet her.

"You poor child, come here with me," Mae crooned to her as she tucked Jessie's hand in the crook of her elbow and led her into the house.

"I feel like I have finally arrived home, Aunt Mae." Jessie smiled.